the incredible worlds of W9-ATA-216

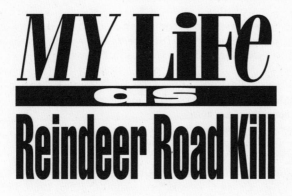

MY LiFe as Reindeer Road Kill

BILL MYERS

Tommy NELSON®

Thomas Nelson, Inc.

Nashville

Published in Nashville, Tennessee, by Tommy Nelson®, a
division of Thomas Nelson, Inc. Visit us on the Web at
www.tommynelson.com

Cover art by Jonathan Gregerson.

Scripture quotations are from the *International Children's
Bible®, New Century Version®*, copyright © 1986, 1988, 1999 by
Tommy Nelson®, a division of Thomas Nelson, Inc.

Library of Congress Cataloging-in-Publication Data

Myers, Bill, 1953–
    My life as reindeer road kill / Bill Myers.
        p.   cm. — (The incredible worlds of Wally McDoogle ; bk. #9)
    Summary: Wally receives an invitation to the Lord's birthday
party on December 25 and bungles his way to understanding
the best gift to give God.
    ISBN 0–8499–3866–X
    [1. Christmas—Fiction. 2. Christian life—Fiction.
3. Humorous stories.] I. Title. II. Series: Myers, Bill, 1953–   .
Incredible worlds of Wally McDoogle ; #9.
PZ7.M98234Myj   1995
[Fic]—dc20   95–23714
                                                         CIP
                                                         AC

Printed in the United States of America

03 04 PHX 17 16

For Traci and Randy—
as you grow together in your love,
and in God's.

To Riley

"I tell you the truth. Anything you did for any of my people here, you also did for me."
—Matthew 25:40

Billy Graham

Contents

Chapter 1

Just for Starters . . .

The nice thing about dreams is that you don't have to take them seriously. It doesn't matter what happens. You can fall off the Empire State Building. Or run too slow and become the grease spot on the wheels of a runaway freight train. Or explode from eating one too many peanut butter cups. What difference does it make? You always wake up safe and sound in the morning where the only real worry is who gets to use the bathroom next.

At least that's what I used to think. But not any more. . . .

It all started innocently enough two nights before Christmas. I was dreaming about all the cool stuff I'd be getting. In the dream I was hanging out in some motorbike shop signing autographs for the latest movie I was starring in (okay, I like to dream big) and checking out all the jet-powered

1

motorcycles Mom wanted to give me for Christmas (okay, I like to dream *real* big).

Suddenly, this guy in a white tuxedo, top hat, and black cane appeared at the front of the line. "Good day, Wallace," he said in a thick English accent.

"Who are you?"

"Allow me to introduce myself. My name is Bartholomew. I am your guardian angel."

"That's nice," I said, reaching for another one of my photos to sign for him. "So tell me Bart, do I make this out to you, or to your boss?"

Before he could answer, the man behind him growled, "Back of the line, punk." I looked up and saw the famous movie star Clint Westwood grabbing the guy by the shoulders. "When it comes to getting Mr. McDoogle's autograph, we don't take kindly to cuts."

"That's right," a woman's voice agreed. It was Laura Lottalips, star of stage and screen. She was standing right behind Clint, batting her baby blues directly at me. "We've waited over six hours to meet the marvelous Wally McDoogle. I'm afraid you'll just have to wait your turn."

The guy in the tux threw me a grin. "I say, old boy, you certainly know how to dream, don't you?"

I frowned. "What?"

"This is a dream, Wallace. Just another one of your crazy dreams."

"No way."

"Oh really?" he asked, picking up a nearby pizza I'd been munching on. "Since when do they make chocolate-covered pizzas?"

I took a look at the chocolate delight and answered, "Since . . . since . . ." He had a point. I couldn't ever remember eating chocolate-covered pizza.

Suddenly, Bartholomew snapped his fingers and everything froze—people's conversations, Clint's scornful scowl, Laura's baby blue eyes. Everything.

"Hey . . ." I nervously rose to my feet. "How'd you do that?"

"Like I said, old chap, this is merely a dream. In reality you're still back home in bed imagining all of this."

I looked at Clint, then Laura, then all the other superstars, models, and Olympic champions waiting in line for my autograph. "You mean . . . ?"

"Sorry, old bean."

I motioned to the half dozen motorbikes Mom was about to put on her Mastercard. "And those?"

"Same thing."

I sighed heavily. "You sure know how to wreck a good dream."

"Yes, well sometimes it's difficult knowing exactly what's going on in that head of yours."

I gave him a careful look over. "I thought angels had wings and were big and powerful."

"Quite right. I'm just in this disguise so I don't scare you. It can be so embarrassing having you humans keel over from heart attacks when I first meet you."

"So what do you want . . . Mr. uh . . .?"

"Bartholomew. You've received quite an honor, Wallace." He reached into his pocket and produced a small envelope that looked like any other small envelope, except that it was made out of leaping flames of fire.

"Watch it!" I yelled.

"Oh, so sorry." He blew out the flames with one breath. "Go ahead, it's addressed to you."

I finally took the envelope and turned it over. Sure enough, the front had my name printed on it in gold. I opened it and pulled out a small white card. It read:

The Lord requests your presence
for a brief visit at His birthday party
the 25th day of December of this year.

I looked up at him. "This is a joke."

"Nope. A dream."

"I mean this card."

"Wrong again."

"You're kidding."

"Angels don't kid, although we do enjoy a good laugh now and then, especially over those old Gilligan's Island reruns."

"But . . . but . . . but," I stuttered, doing my best motorboat imitation. "Where . . . ? How . . . ?"

"I'll take care of the details. But be prepared. I may be back as early as tomorrow night."

"But that's only the 24th."

"Yes, well, with holiday traffic being what it is these days, I'd like us to get an early start." He glanced at his pocket watch. "Well, I must be off."

"But . . . wait a minute. . . ."

He tapped his black cane on the ground twice and began to disappear before my very eyes.

I talked faster. "If it's His birthday, shouldn't I bring Him a birthday present or something?"

"An excellent observation Wallace. A birthday gift would be most appropriate." He had nearly vanished.

"But . . . but . . . I mean, what do I get? What can a guy get the Creator of the Universe for His birthday?"

By now Bartholomew had completely disappeared. Only his voice remained. "Oh, I'm quite positive you'll think of something. Ta-ta."

Suddenly I bolted up in bed. It took a minute for me to get my bearings. Wow, talk about realistic. I took a deep breath and slowly let it out.

Well, the important thing was it was only a dream. No bike shop, no autograph line, and, best of all, no Bartholomew.

I shook my head and muttered, "I tell you, McDoogle, you've got to stop eating so many anchovies on your ice cream before going to bed." I threw off the covers and staggered to my feet. Talk about weird.

Little did I know that the weirdness had barely begun. . . .

* * * * *

I stumbled down to the kitchen, where our family breakfast circus was in full swing. There were Burt and Brock, my twin, superjock brothers. They've been growing about a foot per week so instead of spoons and bowls, they just open their mouths and cram in whatever's in reach. I don't want to say they eat like animals (let alone, tell you what type), but let's just say it's hard to hear yourself think over all their gruntings, snortings, and oinkings.

I pulled up a chair as my six-year-old sister, Carrie, went into her usual hysteria over one food group touching another.

"But honey," Mom said, "I've already put the milk on your Wheaties. You can't separate them now."

"Wipe them off; wipe them off."

"Honey, they're already soaked."

"Couldn't you put them in the clothes dryer?" she pleaded.

Mom stood dazed. I could see Carrie had stumped her.

Fortunately, Brock came to her rescue. "Don't be stupid," he said between mouthfuls of food. "You can't put Wheaties in the dryer."

"Why not?" Carrie demanded.

"Because."

Now for Brock, that was real deep thinking and an outstanding use of logic.

But Carrie was not about to give up so easily. "Because, why?"

Brock frowned. That about wrapped it up for him in the thinking department. But that was okay. Burt was nearby and as the Einstein of the two, he always had an answer. "Because, silly, if you put them in the dryer, they'll shrink and you'll have to eat twice as many."

"Oh," Carrie said, suddenly seeing the light.

Beside me, Dad was concentrating on a carefully sketched diagram.

"What're you doing?" I asked, reaching for a box of cereal and discovering it was as empty as the first two I'd tried. (Burt and Brock were growing faster than I thought.)

"My new Christmas outdoor lighting plan."

Everyone at the table froze. We all knew Dad had the world's worst taste when it came to decorating with outdoor Christmas lights. I don't want to say it's bad, but last year we had three bomb threats and one offer by the Middleton Art Museum to put the entire house on display in their Modern Art wing.

Basically, Dad's ability to tastefully decorate the house with Christmas lights rated right up there with my ability to go through an entire day without a major mishap. Mathematically speaking, the odds were:

1 : no way, no how, forget it

But you couldn't convince Dad of that. And this year he was running late getting the lights up.

"With everybody's help, I'm sure we can get it all up in just one afternoon," Dad said.

The family responded immediately: "No way. . . . No how. . . . Forget it."

My brothers and sister all had excuses.

"Me and Burt have to write advertisements for our new outdoor concession stand," Brock said.

"What are you selling now?" I asked.

"Snow cones."

Only my two brothers could dream up such a business in the middle of December, where a blistering high of 15 degrees below zero is expected.

But they've come a long way compared to their last business venture . . . selling toothbrushes to the toothless:

> *"Just think of our savings by not having to include bristles," Brock had said.*
> *"Yeah," Burt agreed, "and if we don't have bristles, who needs handles to hold them? We can just sell empty cases!"*

Carrie had an even better excuse. "I'd love to help, Daddy, but I have to study my lines for the Christmas pageant."

"Well, son," Dad said, slapping his strong hand on my not-so-strong back, "I guess it's just you and me."

After finishing my coughing fit, readjusting my spine, and crawling back up on the chair, I did what any loyal, loving son without an excuse would do. I desperately tried to change the subject. "Hey, Mom, whatcha' watching?"

Mom was watching television while she slaved over something on the kitchen counter (a position she stayed in from Thanksgiving until sometime after New Year's). To help ease the boredom, she usually had a little black-and-white portable TV blaring.

"Oh, it's one of those old musicals," she laughed. "Something silly about a boy being invited to some king's party."

The plot seemed strangely familiar, though I couldn't put my finger on it. I pushed up my glasses and squinted at the screen. There was some guy dancing around in a white tuxedo, top hat, and black cane.

"So what do you say?" Dad asked me hopefully. "Just you and me?"

I gave Dad a smile while straining to listen to the TV. The guy in the tux had a British accent. "Go ahead, old bean," he was saying to the boy, "open the envelope."

Dad continued, "Father and son."

"It's an invitation to attend the king's birthday party," the guy in the tux said.

"Sort of a male-bonding thing," Dad glowed.

"But if it's his birthday," the boy asked, "shouldn't I bring him a present?"

"An excellent observation," Tux Guy said. "A birthday gift would be most appropriate."

"You and me against the elements." Dad was really getting into it.

"But what do you get a king for his birthday?" the boy asked, pushing up his glasses.

"Oh, I am quite positive you'll think of something." With that, he tapped his cane twice, said, "Ta-ta," and instantly vanished.

I stared at the screen. My heart pounded like a jackhammer. How did my dream get on TV?

Or was it a dream?

Could I really have been visited by an angel? Was this some sort of sign, his way of telling me he was really for real?

"So, it's settled," Dad said, grinning from ear to ear. "We'll get started as soon as I dig out the lights from the garage."

"Sure, Dad," I said, barely hearing him. "Whatever you say."

"Great," he slapped me on the back again. "This will be just great."

I crawled back onto the chair, not so sure anything was going to be great.

Chapter 2

Another Sign

Thanks to all the junk we'd thrown in the garage over the year, it was going to take Dad a "couple of months" to dig out the lights. So in the meantime, I headed up to my room to figure out what to do. If my dream was real, then I should start shopping for a birthday gift. Christmas was in two days, but according to Bartholomew I should have everything ready tonight, just in case. I calmly glanced at my watch. That would give me . . . *LESS THAN 12 HOURS!* (That about wrapped it up for being calm.)

I tried to relax and think through my options. What if the movie on TV was just a coincidence? If that were true, then I'd look like a total fool.

Actually, looking like a total fool didn't bother me much. That was one of my specialties. It was the other possibility that had me worried, the one where I might show up in heaven with no gift or, worse yet, some lame, last-minute present. I mean, let's face it, buying a birthday gift for God's Only Son is not like buying something for your dad. You can't just get Him a pair of socks or a tie or golf balls. It has to be something a little fancier.

To help me think through all this, I took out ol' Betsy, my laptop computer. When a guy wants to clear his mind, I have found that nothing helps like writing a good superhero story. I opened up the lid, snapped it on, and went to work. . . .

"Wake up, Bubble Boy. Rise and pop."
Bubblegum Man McDoogle stirs in his gum wrapper and tries to go back to sleep, but it does little good. His mother turns on the lights and begins to shake him.

"Come on, now. It's almost Christmas, and you've got a whole world of bad guys just waiting to be chewed up and spit out. Time to get snapping and popping."

Of course his mom is right. At the moment he is the nation's only avail-able superhero. Batman, Superman, and all those other hot shots are too busy making movies to be of any help. Not that Bubblegum Man hadn't tried to get into pictures, but for some reason the producers thought handsome men in masks and flying capes were more appealing than a giant wad of used bubblegum. Showbiz, go figure.

Bubblegum Man McDoogle stretches his pink, stringy arms and yawns. "What's on the schedule this morning, Ma?"

His mother reads the appointment calendar:

> 9:00 A.M.—Save a runaway space
> shuttle.

"Again?" he groans. "That's the third time this month."

"I know, but ever since your friend, Wally, went up as an afterthought astronaut, things have gotten out of hand."

Bubblegum Man nods. "Then what?"

> 9:15 A.M.—Gum-chewing lessons
> for the President. Teach him
> to walk at the same time.
>
> 9:30 A.M.—Save the world.

9:45 A.M.——Hot chocolate break.

"Now remember, son," his mother
warned. "Don't drink your chocolate too
hot——you know how heat makes you all
runny and gooey."
"Yes, Mother," Bubblegum Man sighs.
"You tell me that every day."
"You know how I worry. You may be the
world's greatest superhero to everybody else," she gives his cheek a small
pinch, "but you're still Momma's little
bubble boy."
Bubblegum Man groans.
Mom continues:

10:00 A.M.——Give speech to
Abandoned Wads Anonymous
about the rising epidemic of
chewing gum left under school
desks.

11:00 A.M.——Film a commercial
for the Society for the
Prevention of Cruelty to
Chewing Gum.

"Is that one where I tell kids not to

chew gum and eat popcorn at the same time?"

Mom nods. "Otherwise it turns the gum into grainy goop."

Bubblegum Man shudders. "What a way to go."

No one's sure why his mom gave birth to a nine-pound, six-ounce wad of bubblegum instead of a baby boy. But Bubblegum Man is her only son and nothing can stop her from loving him. She knows that underneath that colorful wrapper and powdery pink exterior lies a heart of gold (with your choice of grape, strawberry, or regular flavors).

Some say she had swallowed one too many pieces of bubblegum when she was pregnant. Others blame it on Bubblegum Man's father, who was an avid baseball card collector. He left all those slabs of gum lying around—the ones you used to have to buy to get the cards. Then there's the ever popular theory that Wally McDoogle, the author of these stories, just thought it would be cool to have a piece of bubblegum for a hero.

Whatever the reason, Mom loved her bubblegum son and taught him to walk (not an easy task with such sticky feet)...to eat (no problem as long as he stayed away from liquids and solids)...and to breathe (without turning himself into the world's biggest bubble).

Suddenly the Bubble Phone rings.

Bubblegum Man stretches his arm across the room and picks it up. "Hello, Crime Chewers. We take a bite out of crime ...and keep right on chewing."

"Moo-who-who-ha-ha-he-he!"

Bubblegum Man recognizes the voice instantly. It is the husky and heavy-handed voice of...TA-TA-DA! (that's the bad-guy music)...Gravity Guy.

"Gravity Guy," our hero shouts, "is that you?"

The voice on the other end cackles. "Of course it is. Didn't you just hear the bad-guy music? I wanted you to be the first to know."

"Know what?"

"That I've just completed my Anti-Gravity Generator."

"You've what?"

"You heard me, Bubble Brain."

"But that's impossible."

"Oh really?" There was a loud crackle on the other end followed by even more bad-guy laughter and bad-guy music.

Suddenly, Bubblegum Man feels as light as a feather. The explanation is simple—he IS as light as a feather. In fact, he's actually floating off the ground.

He spins around to his mother. She is starting to float, too. "Wow," she cries in delight, "that new diet is really paying off."

"Gravity Guy!" our hero shouts into the phone. "What have you done?"

"Oh, I bet you can figure it out."

"But what do you want? How can I stop you?"

"If I tell you now, your readers won't have to keep reading."

"You mean..."

"That's right, you won't know 'til the next section of this little story. Moo-who-who-ha-ha-he-he..."

I stared at the screen. Was it my imagination or were these stories getting weirder? Before I could decide, Mom called from downstairs.

"Wally, can you go to the store for me? I need you to pick up some popcorn."

I sighed and in my best whine shouted. "Aw, Mom . . ."

"If we're stringing popcorn for the tree tonight, I need to get it popped."

So much for my best whine. Mom was pretty flexible about a lot of stuff, but there was one thing you didn't mess with her about . . . Family Christmas-Tree Decorating.

Each year the whole family would get together and decorate the tree. It was a group thing. Earlier in the week Burt, Brock, and Dad had gone tree hunting. (I wanted to tag along, but since that would mean being near sharp objects like an ax, they insisted I stay home.)

Then a night or two before Christmas, Mom would play carols on the piano while the rest of us strung popcorn, scarfed down the Christmas goodies she'd baked, and put up all the lights and ornaments. It was a pretty cool tradition, and we all liked it. But not Mom. She *loved* it. There was a lot you could get away with if you pouted and sulked and complained, but no one, I mean *no one*, messed with Mom's night of Family Christmas-Tree Decorating.

I pressed F10 to save the story and shut ol' Betsy down. Gravity Guy was right. I guess I'd have to wait for the next time.

* * * * *

Shopping for Mom is definitely not on my list of all-time favorite things to do—especially when I should probably be picking up a little something for God's Only Son, instead. But I still wasn't entirely convinced on the whole angel routine. And since the store was only a few blocks away, I figured, *What could it hurt?*

I'd obviously slipped into a mild case of brain deadness. The phrase "What could it hurt" always has an answer, at least for me. In fact, the answer usually was *me.* Yes sir, you don't work all those years to earn the title "Human Disaster Area" by letting normal everyday situations like going shopping for your mother slip by. Not without working in a few catastrophes along the way. After all, a guy's got a reputation to keep up.

At the beginning, everything went pretty smoothly. I'd picked up the popcorn and a few other items for Mom at Hockeldorf's Supermarket. As I checked out, I kept thinking about the dream. Was Bartholomew for real? Could the movie on Mom's TV have been a sign? Or was it all just some weird coincidence? The only way to tell for sure was to wait for another sign. Something bigger and better—something that would really get my attention.

I was still so busy thinking about this stuff that,

as I left the store, I almost ran into a little old lady. The good news was I missed her. The bad news was I didn't miss her poodle. I stepped on the pooch's perfectly manicured tootsies, and the thing went ballistic. It yelped and howled and carried on worse than Burt trying to sing in the shower.

"Poodikens!" the old lady screamed.

"I'm sorry!" I shouted. I jumped back and crashed into a row of trash cans. Of course the cans went falling to the sidewalk, and of course, I followed right behind.

Normally this would be enough for your average, run-of-the-mill catastrophe, but being the world-class champion of chaos that I am, I knew people would be expecting much more. So, I'd barely hit the sidewalk when I felt another sensation. Poodikens had sunk his needle-sharp pearlies into my leg.

"YEOW!" I cried. I scrambled through the spilled cans and leaped up. Unfortunately, Wonder Mutt was still attached to my leg. Unfortunatelier, my leap sent me flying out of the pile and right into the bottom section of someone's passing shopping cart. Unfortunateliest, that someone's baby was sitting in the upper section.

I landed on the cart with such force that we all flew back into Hockeldorf's store through the automatic doors.

"Poodikens!" screamed the old lady.

"My baby!" screamed the young mother.

"Oh, no!" screamed me. (The reason was simple. I had just spotted my next victim. An upcoming display of Christmas Party Mix.)

BAMB!

Party Mix flew everywhere.

"Poodikens!" screamed the old lady.

"My baby!" screamed the young mother.

"My Party Mix!" screamed Mr. Hockeldorf.

"Cough, cough, gasp, gasp," choked me.

But we weren't done, yet. Not quite. Wonder Mutt kept hanging onto my leg while wildly kicking his back feet against the floor, which only propelled us faster. We did a few figure eights before making a U-turn.

Next stop, the dairy counter. Fortunately, there were no displays to knock over. Just eggnog cartons that Baby on Board thought would be cool to reach out and knock down.

Klunk, splash.

"OW!"

Klunk, splash; klunk, splash.

"Will you stop—"

Klunk, splash; klunk, splash; klunk, splash.

"knocking those—"

Klunk, splash; klunk, splash; klunk, splash; klunk, splash.

"cartons on me!"

At last, the check-out counter came back into view.

What luck!

And beyond that, the automatic doors and the busy street intersection.

What horror!

People leaped out of the way as we zoomed through the check-out line and past the cashier.

"Poodikens!"

"My baby!"

"My Party Mix!"

"Will that be cash or credit?"

And then, just like that, we stopped. Well, everybody else stopped. We'd hit the outside handrail along the doors. Well, the cart, the baby, and Poodikens hit the outside handrail. I shot out from under the cart and began a human bobsled imitation, sliding across the icy sidewalk and out into the middle of the busy intersection.

Cars honked. Tires skidded.

I fainted.

When I came to, a black cane was poking me in the ribs. My eyes widened in horror as I recognized it from Mom's TV movie . . . and my dream! Some old-timer kept jabbing me with it and ranting: "Pay attention to the signs! Pay attention to the signs!"

Of course he was probably screaming about the

"No Walk" sign he kept jerking his thumb toward. Or was he? Could he also be talking about another sign . . . the type sent First Class by angels from heaven?

I didn't stick around to find out. I scrambled to my feet and raced home as fast as my bruised and battered body could carry me. All the time the old geezer kept screaming, "Pay attention to the signs; pay attention to the signs!"

If this was Bartholomew's way of getting my attention, he'd gotten it.

Big time.

Chapter 3

A Plan of Action

I wasn't home more than 3.2 seconds before I called up Opera, my best friend, and Wall Street, my other best friend. Since time was running out, they agreed to rush over to my place for an emergency meeting of Dork-oids Anonymous (of which I, of course, am President). Unfortunately, they arrived just in time for Dad to ask us to help with the lights he had strung all over the front yard.

Since they were the old-fashioned lights, that meant somebody had to go through and tighten each bulb. And since we were the nearest some-bodies, and since I'd already agreed to help him, that meant holding our little Dork-oid meeting in the freezing outdoors. I don't want to say it was cold out there, but the snowman I had built was already turning blue.

"Okay, kids," Dad called from the driveway.

"Just work your way down this line of lights toward the garage. I have to go out and find some new fasteners so we can attach them to the eaves."

We nodded as he climbed in the car and took off.

"So you really think it was an angel?" Opera shouted over the Walkman headphones that were permanently attached to his ears. The guy had two passions, classical music and junk food. Right now, in honor of the holidays, he was listening to Pavarotti singing the Chipmunk Christmas song. He was also working on his second bag of deep-fried, salt-saturated, artery-plugging potato chips.

"I don't know if it was an angel or not," I shouted back. "But if it was, what am I supposed to buy Jesus for a birthday present?"

Opera shrugged. "That could get real expensive."

"And don't forget the postage," Wall Street added. "Imagine how much it costs to mail a package to heaven these days." Unlike Opera, Wall Street only had one love, money. As someone who wanted to make her first million by age fourteen, money was the only thing she thought of.

"I'm not mailing the gift," I said. "I'm taking it. In person."

"Then I hope He's paying for the airline tickets. Those holiday fares can be murder."

"I don't know the details. I don't even know if

it's real! I mean how many people have ever been invited to a birthday party for God's Son?"

"Good point," Opera shouted.

"It's crazy," I said.

"Uh-huh."

"Absurd."

"Yup."

"It's just not normal."

"Aren't you forgetting one thing?" Wall Street asked.

"What's that?"

"*You're* not normal."

"She's got you there," Opera agreed. "If it's crazy, absurd, and not normal . . . that makes you the guy for the job."

I sighed. "So it's probably all real, isn't it?"

They looked at me and nodded.

We continued tightening the bulbs, working our way closer and closer to the laundry room in the garage. "So what do I get Him?"

"It better be good," Wall Street said.

"And it better be soon," I added. "What if the angel shows up tonight and I don't have anything?"

Suddenly Opera snapped his fingers. "I've got it! How 'bout a year's supply of fruitcake?"

"I'm not sure," I frowned. "I know Jesus is supposed to be forgiving and all, but wouldn't fruitcake push Him over the edge?"

Wall Street nodded. "It's got to be something *really* classy."

"Which means *really* expensive," I groaned.

She nodded.

"And I'm flat broke."

"No sweat," Opera shouted. "I can get you a job over at Pederson's Hobby and Sporting Goods Store."

"Are you playing Santa in their live window display again?" I asked.

"That's right, and we need more reindeer."

"How much do they pay?"

"Four dollars and fifty cents an hour."

I moaned.

"But they throw in all the Trail Mix you can eat!"

I moaned louder.

We had reached the end of the light string. Now it was time to plug it in. Wall Street followed me as I picked up the plug and headed to the laundry room just off the garage.

"Don't worry, Wally," she said, trying to comfort me. "I'll float you a loan."

My heart soared. What a friend, what a pal.

"Of course I'll have to charge you interest."

My heart crashed. What a con artist, what a user. It's true, Wall Street was on her way to making that first million. The only problem was that, so far, most of that money had been made off yours truly.

"Relax," she grinned. "It won't be too painful. We'll work out some sort of payment plan."

I tried to smile, but I already suspected her payment plan would mean giving up any car I'd ever own, the mortgage to whatever house I'd ever buy, and, of course, the birthrights of all the children I'd ever have.

We arrived at the electrical outlet. There was just one problem. Actually two. There were two receptacles. One was labeled 110. The other 220. Which one were we supposed to use?

"What do you think?" I asked.

"You can plug it into the 110 to be safe," she offered, "but that might make them too dim. Or you can plug it into the 220 and really light up the place."

She had a point. And, being a live-on-the-edge, ever-so-macho, courageous type of guy (hey, everybody needs a little fantasy in his life), I went for the 220. Suddenly I heard a loud popping sound, accompanied by Opera screaming his head off.

We raced back out to the yard to see one bulb after another blow up. The explosions worked their way down the line like little firecrackers, until the last bulb finally went off.

I stood in stunned silence watching the smoke slowly rise from the wires.

"Looks like I'll be loaning you a little extra for Christmas bulbs, too," Wall Street offered.

* * * * *

Once Dad got back home and finished his lecture on electrical wiring, he let me take off. "The important thing is you tried, son, and I appreciate that."

"If you want, I can stay behind a little longer and—"

"No way!" he blurted. Then, catching himself, he tried to sound a bit more in control. "That is to say, I think you've been more than enough help already, Wally."

I looked from him to the shattered glass and smoldering wires in the front yard. Maybe he had a point.

"Okay," I said. "If you're sure."

"I'm sure," he replied. "Believe me, I'm sure."

Wall Street, Opera, and I headed toward the house when Opera glanced at his watch. "I've got to go."

"What's up?" I asked.

"I've got to catch the bus to the Sporting Goods Store. I replace the daytime Santa at three. Sure you don't want to come?"

"No thanks," I said. "Somehow I suspect I'm going to need a little more than $4.50 an hour."

"Don't forget the Trail Mix," he said. "We're not

just talking dried fruit and peanuts, we're talking dried fruit and *honey-glazed* peanuts."

I could almost see the saliva dripping out his mouth. "No thanks, Opera. I think I'll pass."

"Your loss," he said. Then, turning up Pavarotti to a level just above *This-Should-Make-Your-Eyes-Water*, he sauntered down the driveway singing something about only wanting a Hula-Hoop for Christmas.

Wall Street and I headed into the kitchen. As usual for this time of year, Mom was up to her elbows in cookie dough.

"Sweetheart, I've got some bad news."

I froze in my tracks, afraid that Bartholomew had made another guest appearance.

"We'll have to postpone our tree decorating until Christmas Eve."

"What happened?" I asked in concern.

"Your brothers," she threw a look to Burt and Brock sitting at the kitchen table. "They have some sort of meeting tonight, something about their new business. We'll have to put off decorating the tree until Christmas Eve. I hope you're not too disappointed."

"Nah," I said. "Besides, Wall Street and I have some last minute shopping today."

"Really? For whom?"

For the briefest second I thought of telling her about my dream, about Bartholomew, and about

the little sign I'd received that morning while
shopping for her. But then I figured you could
really ruin a parent's holiday by telling them their
son was nuttier than a bag of peanuts. Before I
could come up with a better answer, Wall Street
interrupted.

"Those Christmas cookies sure smell great," she
said. "Have you ever thought about marketing
them, Mrs. McDoogle? I know an investor in New
York who specializes in franchises, and I bet he
could—"

"I don't think so, Wall Street," Mom smiled.
"This is just a Christmas tradition for my family.
Oh, Wally, one other thing."

"Yeah?"

"I received a call from Mr. Hockeldorf at the
supermarket."

"Uh-huh . . ."

"He was so impressed by you at his store this
morning that he asked if he could home deliver
our groceries for the rest of the year."

"Home deliver our groceries?"

"That's right. Of course I said it wasn't neces-
sary and that you were more than willing to go
down and pick things up for me, but . . ."

"But what?"

"Well, the poor man practically broke into tears.
He kept begging me to let him personally deliver

anything we needed to our house. Isn't that fantastic? I tell you, that's one man who really understands the spirit of the Season."

I nodded, knowing it wasn't so much his Christmas Cheer as it was his McDoogle Fear. Mr. Hockeldorf was obviously trying to keep his store in one piece, at least through the holidays.

Over at the kitchen table, Burt and Brock were still bruising their brains over the advertisement for their outdoor snow-cone stand. "Hey Wally," Burt shouted. "What rhymes with 'Frostbitten Teeth?'"

I hesitated, "Uh, guys, are you sure you're heading in the right direction with this thing?"

"See, I told you," Brock said, knocking Burt along the side of the head. "Teeth don't get frostbite. It's got to be tongue . . . we've got to find a phrase to rhyme with 'Frostbitten Tongue.' Thanks, Wally."

"Don't mention it," I said, then quietly mumbled, "to anyone."

I pushed open the kitchen door and entered the dining room. Carrie was busy rehearsing her lines with Collision, our family cat. Now, as you may recall, Collision did not get her name because of her lucky breaks. Actually it had more to do with *UN*lucky breaks . . . legs, paws, tail. You name it, she's broken it. The best we can figure it has something to do with her timing . . . like choosing to sleep in the dryer on wash days, or snuggling up nice and close to the fan belt in Dad's car just before he drives off to work.

"Hello, Wally." Carrie's voice had all the excitement of wilted lettuce.

"What's up, Squirt?"

"Collision's not cooperating." She pointed to the chandelier above the dining room table. For some reason Carrie had unscrewed all of the bulbs from their fixtures and had set Collision up there where the poor cat was hanging on for dear life.

"Why'd you put Collision on the chandelier?" I asked.

"She's supposed to be the Angel of the Lord."

"The what?" I asked, feeling a twinge of panic over the word angel.

"You know, the one that appears to the shepherds and announces the birth of the Savior."

"Of course," I nodded. "And you took out all the bulbs because . . . ?"

"Because it's supposed to be night."

"I see." I thought of suggesting it would be easier to turn off the switch, but I knew better than to mess with a six-year-old's logic.

"She just hangs there crying and whining," Carrie scowled. "Angels don't cry and whine. They sing and talk in big voices."

"They also do great dances with top hats and canes."

"What?"

"Never mind. Listen, Carrie, maybe Collision doesn't want to be an angel. Why don't you take her down," I suggested. "I'll help you with your lines when I get back."

"Promise?"

"Sure."

She wrapped her arms around me. "You're the greatest."

"Come on!" Wall Street motioned impatiently from the doorway into the kitchen. "If we're hitting my bank and getting a gift before the stores close, then we'd better hurry."

"You really think we can find something?" I asked.

"Hey, with my money and a little luck, no sweat."

We raced for the door. Of course, I thought of reminding her how well luck and I don't get along, but I figured we'd been through enough adventures for her to remember. Then again, if she'd forgotten, I was sure there would be plenty of opportunities to refresh her memory. . . .

Chapter 4

Shopping Spree

Other than the usual staggerings and fallings, the trip to Wall Street's bank was pretty uneventful—except for that problem with the bell-ringing Santa. I didn't see him until I accidentally knocked him into the passing skateboarder, who accidentally fell off, just as Santa fell on the skateboard and rolled down the wrong way of a one-way street full of semitrucks.

After helping the shaking Santa into the ambulance, we resumed our journey and arrived at the bank. If the phrase "Money talks" ever had meaning, it was here, inside Wall Street's bank. But it wasn't so much Wall Street's money that was talking. It was all of the people who handled her money. As soon as we had walked through the doors, everyone was all friendly chit-chats and smiles.

From the front guard: "Merry Christmas, Ms. Wall Street."

To the teller: "Season's Greetings, Ms. Wall Street."

To the Vice President with the fancy suit: "Making another deposit are we, Ms. Wall Street?"

"Not today," she grinned. "Today I've come to close out my account."

Suddenly everything in the bank froze . . . including Mr. Fancy Suit's smile. If money could talk, it was suddenly suffering from a bad case of laryngitis. Nobody moved. Nobody spoke. Finally, Fancy Suit cleared his throat while trying unsuccessfully to stop his right cheek from twitching. "I'm sorry, Ms. Wall Street, did you say you wished to *close* your account?"

"That's right. I'm taking out all my money to go Christmas shopping for my friend here."

Every eye turned from Wall Street to me. I wish I could say their expressions were full of Season's Greetings, but it looked more like Yuletide Chill. It's not that they were angry, but if looks could kill, I'd be expecting to find a nice little electric chair under my Christmas tree.

"Wall Street," I whispered. "How much money do you have in this place?"

"Enough," she grinned.

"Ah . . . Ms. Wall Street . . ." Fancy Suit croaked

as if he'd just swallowed a box of soda crackers and washed them down with a nice, big glass of sand. "May I see you for a moment?" he asked. *"Privately."*

"No sweat," she said.

Now if I remember my lessons in high finance, banks love to keep your money so they can loan it out to other people and charge them interest. That's how they stay in business. A pretty good plan until somebody with a lot of dough takes it all out. That's how they go *out* of business.

It's really a lot more complicated than that, but by the looks on all the employees' faces, I figured that was a good enough guess. I looked down to the ground, feeling their eyes bore into me. I pretended to busy myself with something, but there's only so many times you can count the shoelace holes in your Reeboks before you get a little bored. Finally I heard Wall Street's voice.

"Okay, Wally, let's get going."

I looked up, and quickly followed her toward the door.

"Good-bye, Ms. Wall Street."

"Happy Holidays, Ms. Wall Street."

"Merry Christmas, Ms. Wall Street."

"How much money did you have stashed in there, anyway?" I asked as we headed down the street. "How much did you take out?"

"Oh, I left a few hundred thousand behind," she grinned.

I choked. "A few hundred thousand . . . DOLLARS? How much are we planning to spend?"

"Don't worry," she smiled. "We've got enough."

"But . . . how . . . much?" Suddenly my voice sounded as dry as Fancy Suit's.

"Let's just say you and I are going to make this one of Jesus' better birthdays."

I hoped so. Because the way my heart was going into triple overtime, there was a good chance I'd be spending a lot more time with Jesus a lot sooner than I thought.

Unfortunately, we'd only just begun. . . .

* * * * *

Since the mall had the greatest number of ways to spend money in the shortest amount of time, we decided on it. We didn't have much time, so Wall Street shifted into something Mom and Carrie are pros at . . . "Hyperdrive Buying."

First stop:

PAYMORE DEPARTMENT S ORE

It used to be "*STORE*," but people keep ripping

off the "T" from the sign. And, at their send-you-into-open-heart-surgery kind of prices, I could see why people were "sore."

"Where're we going?" I shouted as we raced through the appliance section.

"Hardware Department!" she cried.

A moment later we stood panting and out of breath, surrounded by more hammers, chisels, and drills than my dentist's office.

"Why here?"

"Wasn't He a carpenter or something?" she asked, searching the aisles.

"Who?"

"Jesus."

"Well yeah, but—"

"There it is! Perfect!" She pointed to a tablesaw the size of the USS Kitty Hawk. And, luckily, it was on sale for roughly half the price of a real aircraft carrier.

"I don't know," I said. "Do you think He does that sort of work anymore?"

"Got me," she said. "If it's not right, you can always return it."

Before I could answer, she dished out the cash to a sales clerk and gave careful instructions on how to deliver the tablesaw to my house (with a 30% tip to make sure they'd get it there tonight).

"Thirty percent?" I cried, trying to swallow. But my mouth was as dried up as my bank account . . . from now until the year 2091. "Isn't thirty percent a little steep?"

"Hey, you're the one who waited 'til the last minute to have that dream. Come on."

"Now where?"

"If the tablesaw's not right, you need to have a back-up plan. Come on, let's hurry!"

Soon, we were standing inside:

SHELBY'S SHELL-OUT-THE-DOUGH SHOE STORE

"What do you think of these?" she asked, holding up a pair of $95, calfskin sandals.

I shook my head. "I don't think He's into sandals anymore. The way He gets around these days, He probably needs—" and then I spotted them. "Yes!"

A moment later we were ringing up a pair of *Air* Jordan's.

"Are you sure you've got the right size?" Wall Street asked.

"I, uh, that is to say, um . . . 'size'?"

She turned to the clerk, "Better make that a pair of each size."

"Yes ma'am," giggled the clerk (who was obviously working on commission).

Seconds later we were standing in front of:

BARELY THERE SWIMSUITS

"No way," I insisted. "He doesn't need swim trunks."

"Why not?"

"He doesn't swim in water, He walks on it."

"Good point. Come on!"

Next stop:

GO FOR BROKE FURNISHINGS

It only took Wall Street 1.6 seconds to find the most expensive recliner in the furniture store. Not only did it have a heater and vibrator, but it also had a built-in TV remote, popcorn popper, foot soaker, salami slicer, and Cheese Whiz spreader.

"I don't know," I said, glancing at a price tag that had a number followed by more zeros than the national debt. "I think He's partial to thrones."

"What about His days off? When He wants to kick back and watch TV?"

Our eyes widened in unison. "TV!!"

But by the time we had arrived at:

STEAL U BLIND STEREOS,

I was already having second thoughts. "Do you really think He needs a 720-inch screen?" I asked.

"What if He invites the angels over to watch a game? Heaven's a big place, you know."

"I'm not sure, Wall Street. With what's on TV these days, I don't know if there's *anything* He'd want to watch."

Of course we went ahead and bought it anyway . . . just in case. Along with a VCR, CD player, palm recorder, and anything else that cost just over a small fortune.

Finally nine o'clock rolled around and the mall closed. We were so beat (and broke) that I was glad to call it quits. But still, something wasn't quite right. Maybe it was knowing I'd have to explain to Dad why all the delivery trucks were unloading in our driveway. Maybe it was something else.

Whatever the case, with bedtime and dreamland fast approaching, I expected that if there was a problem, I'd soon find out. . . .

Chapter 5

Calling All Angels . . .

By the time I got home, Mom and Dad were both in bed. I guess Mom was tired from all her baking and preparation for tomorrow night's big tree decorating bash. And by the look of the Christmas lights outside, Dad had again outdone himself in the poor taste department. I don't want to say the place looked bad. But if you've ever seen the millions of cobwebs in those old haunted house movies, and if you can picture those cobwebs being strings of Christmas lights plastered all across the front of your house . . . well, you are getting close.

But, thanks to my little shopping spree, a lot of Dad's handiwork was blocked from our neighbors' view. Everything I had ordered was delivered, stacked, and covered with huge tarps in our driveway.

I climbed over my junk to the front door. It took a moment to squeeze and squirm my way through all the strings of lights, but I finally made it inside.

"Wow," Carrie said as I entered. "You sure know how to shop. Is all that stuff for me?"

I gave her a look.

She shrugged, "I thought I'd give it a shot." She tailed me across the living room. "So who's it really for?"

I didn't bother to answer. "What'd Dad say about it?"

"He says it's all going back tomorrow."

I nodded. "Hopefully it won't be here by then." I headed toward the kitchen for a late night munchie. Carrie stayed at my side, continuing her human shadow imitation. I pushed open the kitchen door and came to a stop. "What's this?" I asked, pointing to a huge crate in the middle of the floor.

"Mom couldn't find the popcorn you bought, so she ordered some more from Hockeldorf's Supermarket."

I crossed to the crate that was almost as tall as I was. "And he sent this much over because . . ." I already had my answer, but I thought I'd ask anyway.

"Because he was afraid we might run out and Mom might send you to his store again."

I smiled. It pays to have a reputation.

"Wally, are you going to help me with my lines now?"

"Lines?"

"My lines for the Christmas pageant. It's tomorrow night, and I can't—"

"Not now, Squirt," I said, opening the refrigerator and grabbing a three-day-old piece of pizza. "I'm really bushed."

"But my play's tomorrow," she repeated.

I hesitated. There in the door was a can of chocolate syrup. I remembered something about pizza and chocolate syrup in my last dream. I also figured it wouldn't hurt to jump start my dreamer by loading up on weird foods. Don't ask me why, but there's a direct relation between the weirdness of your late-night foods and the weirdness of your dreams.

While I was at it, I also grabbed the Dijon mustard, dill pickles, and, of course, the extra-large bottle of Tabasco sauce. There, if that didn't kick my brain into hyper-dream, nothing would.

"Please . . ." she begged.

"Tomorrow," I said. "I'll help you tomorrow."

She dropped into her little sister sulk, but I couldn't be bothered. I had other things on my mind.

I gobbled down the chocolate-covered pizza and

the mustard/Tabasco sauce pickles (along with some lint-covered cinnamon red hots I'd found in a pocket, just to be safe). Then I crawled into bed. I had to get to sleep and fast.

Unfortunately, my stomach had other ideas. Its rumblings and grumblings were making so much noise that I couldn't sleep.

I smushed up my pillow and turned this way . . . RARRARROROORARAR . . . then that way. WALRAWALRALLALLRWAALALLL . . .

I glanced at the clock: 11:45. I *had* to get to sleep.

Finally, in desperation, I reached for ol' Betsy. Maybe finding what Bubblegum Man was up to would relax me, or at least kill time 'til my stomach quit hollering at me. . . .

When we last left our fat-free and hypoallergenic hero, he was getting a rise from Gravity Guy...literally. Bubblegum Man floats over to the window and looks into the streets. It's worse than he suspects. Cars are floating off the road, groceries are drifting out of shoppers' bags, wads of hundred dollar bills are floating out of beggars' pockets.

Quicker than you can read the part

of this sentence that reads, "quicker
than you can read the part of this sentence," Bubblegum Man stretches his
stringy legs to the floor. In the past
his ultra-sticky feet had always been
an embarrassment. Ice skating was
always a disaster. (It's hard to glide
when you're glued.) Tap dancing was
also an embarrassment. Even his karate
classes were tough, since the opponents
he kicked kept sticking to the bottom
of his feet. But now those sticky feet
were holding him firmly to the ground
and allowing him to race out the door
to his car.

Leaping into the world-famous
Bubblemobile, he fires it up, waits for
the good-guy music to begin, and zooms
off. But where? Where is Gravity Guy
and his Anti-Gravity Generator?

Reaching to his dashboard, Bubblegum
Man snaps on his Anti-Gravity Generator
Tracking Device (the one he installed
for just such emergencies). He races
through the streets searching for
Gravity Guy's hangout, all the time
carefully listening to the homing
device:

> *Beep, beep, beep,* BOP
> *Beep, beep,* BOP
> *Beep,* BOP!
> BOP! CRASH!

He's found it. Of course there is the minor setback of completely totaling his Bubblemobile against the side of the building...and having to squeeze and ooze himself out of the wreckage. (The squeezing and oozing is no problem, but the part where he keeps sticking to the upholstery is a bit of a drag.) Still, those are minor setbacks for someone with such super-sticky stamina.

Ducking the skateboarder flying above the sidewalk and the little old lady desperately looking for the street she had been crossing, Bubblegum Man races to the building's entrance, only to discover...it's actually a bowling alley.

He rushes inside. Everything is chaos. Bowling pins and bowlers are floating in all directions. At the pool table players are sinking eight balls into people's pockets. In the arcade all the Tear-Out-Your-Internal-Organs-and-Eat-Them type video games are bouncing into the ceiling.

"Look out!" someone shouts.

Bubblegum Man spins around just in time to see a bowling ball fly at him faster than a kid channel-surfing past CNN. He leaps aside and the ball whizzes by, barely missing him. Of course, our hero likes bowling as much as the next guy, but he's just not crazy at being mistaken for a pin...especially when someone is trying to pick him up for a spare.

"Moo-who-who-ha-ha-he-he!"

He jumps to his feet and spots...

"Gravity Guy!"

The sinister slimeball is floating beside his giant Anti-Gravity Machine. The device looks so much like it's from an old fifties sci-fi flick that instead of snapping, crackling, and popping, it shakes, rattles, and rolls.

"What do you think of my little invention?" he sneers.

Nobody knows what made Gravity Guy such a bad guy. Some say it was his frustration at being the only 4-foot-2 basketball player in school...especially during jump balls. Others say it was because his English teacher sent him to the office for sitting during the flag salute (when he was standing as tall as he could).

Whatever the cause, before Bubblegum Man can reason with him, Gravity Guy switches two switches, dials three dials, and knobs four knobs.

Instantly, his Anti-Gravity Generator turns into a part-time jet plane (complete with complimentary peanuts and movie on longer flights). He shoots past our hero and out the door.

"Moo-who-who-ha-ha-he-he!"

There is no way to capture this cunningly crafty creep on foot. So before you can say, "Isn't Wally's stomach quiet enough to fall asleep yet?" Bubblegum Man quickly inhales, turning himself into the world's largest bubble. Now, exhaling as fast as he can, he shoots out the door.

Unfortunately, once outside, he runs smack dab into a gazillion gallons of water.

"Gurgle, gurgle, burble, burble!" he cries.

Translation: "Who plugged the sink and left the water running!"

But this is no childhood prank.

It's the local river! With no gravity, the water can't stay in its banks.
That's the bad news. The badder news
is Bubblegum Man can't swim!

"Somebody help!" GLUB!

"Somebody!" GLUB, GLUB!

GLUB, GLUB, GLUB!

Great Scott, who will save our chewy
champion? How will he ever restore
gravity to the earth? And most importantly, when bubblegum dies, does it
go to bubblegum heaven or just stick
on someone's shoe?

I paused to check out my stomach. For the most
part it was done with its grumblings. And, as much
as I wanted to see what would happen to
Bubblegum Man, I was a lot more interested in
the little flight to heaven a certain tap dancing
angel had prepared.

I shut ol' Betsy down, turned off the light, and
waited . . . all the time hoping that Bartholomew
had remembered to get me a round-trip ticket, not
just a one-way.

Chapter 6

A New Plan

"Wally . . . Wally, wake up . . . Wally!"

I felt this finger digging into my ribs. At first I wondered why Bartholomew was trying to perform open-heart surgery on me.

"Wally, it's an emergency. Wally, wake up!"

Then I noticed he wasn't speaking with an English accent. Then I noticed he wasn't even a he. When I finally pried open my eyes I saw that the he was actually a she, and that the she was actually my little sister.

"Wally, we need your help."

"What time is it?" I groaned.

"Almost six. Burt and Brock need you down in the kitchen, fast."

"What?"

"Hurry, before Mom and Dad wake up."

I threw off the covers, leaped to my feet, and fell

to the floor. (Apparently some parts of my body are a little slower at waking up than others.)

I looked around the room. Everything was exactly like it was the night before. Nothing had changed. I grabbed my glasses and looked at the radio alarm. Carrie was right. It was almost six in the morning. A sinking feeling filled my stomach. The entire night had gone by and no Bartholomew. What had gone wrong? Why hadn't he shown up?

I rose and hobbled across the room. After three or four more falls, I finally made it to the window. I looked outside and my heart sank even lower. All the gifts were still stacked in the driveway. Not a thing had been touched. What had happened? After all the trouble I'd gone to, why hadn't he shown up? Weren't they good enough? Had he forgotten?

I was discouraged . . . big time.

"Wally . . . hurry!"

Reluctantly, I followed Carrie down the stairs to find Burt and Brock pushing against the kitchen door. But no matter how hard they pushed to keep it shut, something on the other side kept pushing harder to open it. "What's in there?" I shouted.

"Popcorn!" Burt yelled.

"What?"

"Me and Brock, we took your advice and decided not to sell snow cones. Instead, we're selling popcorn!"

"But how—I mean what—"

"They threw all the popcorn Mr. Hockeldorf gave us into the microwave," Carrie yelled.

"What?" I cried in disbelief.

"We wanted to make sure we had enough."

I started to ask how anybody could be that stupid, but then I remembered who I was talking to and figured I already had my answer. Suddenly the door exploded open.

"LOOK OUT!"

Popcorn poured through the doorway, swirling around our ankles, our knees, rising toward our waists.

"Did you try to shut it off!" I shouted as the kernels rose higher and higher.

"See," Brock cried. "I told you Wally would think of something!"

I sighed my best Why-couldn't-I-have-super-brain-instead-of-superjock-brothers sigh and tried to wade toward the kitchen door. But the current was too strong. The giant, econo-sized, extra fluffy kernels kept pushing me back.

"What do we do?" Burt cried. "We've got to shut it down!"

"I'm going under," I shouted as I took a deep breath and dove headfirst into the raging torrent of corn. Of course, if I'd stopped to remember who I was, I would have realized I could never save the day. That was for my imaginary superheroes, not the real McDoogle. But it was early, and the ol' mind wasn't quite up to speed, so I thought I'd give it a try.

I began to swim.

First the breast stroke, then the Australian crawl, then the back stroke. Nothing seemed to work until I remembered the good, old-fashioned dog paddle. Believe it or not, I actually began to make headway. Soon I was deep in the kitchen, working my way toward the microwave. Behind me I could hear nonstop munching, crunching, and gulping. Without looking, I knew Burt and Brock had devised their own plan for getting through the popcorn.

Paddle, paddle, paddle . . .

I finally arrived at the microwave. The kernels were gushing out like Niagara Falls. No way could I fight against the current and reach the "Off" switch.

Then I saw it. The electrical cord! Suddenly all of Dad's recent electrical training came to mind. I turned and . . .

Paddle, paddle, paddle . . .

I followed the cord to the outlet. Although the current of popcorn was strong, I grabbed the plug and pulled for all I was worth. It suddenly gave way and came out. Instantly, the microwave shut down and the corn slowly stopped popping.

I couldn't believe it. I'd actually done something right. I was actually somebody's hero. I climbed out of the popcorn to join Burt and Brock. I was expecting something: a thank you, a slap on the back, a ticker-tape parade. Anything would do. Unfortunately, they were both looking pretty sick. In fact, for the first time in their lives it looked like they'd actually had enough to eat. Maybe, too much to eat.

"You guys all right?" I asked.

"BURP," said Burt.

"BELCH," said Brock.

"Well, what do we have here?" said Mom.

We all turned to see Mom standing at the door with her hands on her hips.

"BELCH," said Brock.

"BURP," said Burt.

But Mom, always looking on the bright side, just smiled and said, "Well, I guess we'll be stringing a few more strings of popcorn than normal tonight. Unless, of course, you boys are still hungry."

Burt and Brock glanced at each other. Then, in

perfect unison, they covered their mouths and raced for the bathroom.

"Oh, Wally," Mom reached into her robe and handed me a note. "Opera dropped by last night."

I took the note and read:

Wally,
You're wrong about God's gift.
I know what He really wants.
I'll be over first thing tomorrow.

Just then the doorbell rang.

* * * * *

It had taken the whole family and Opera more than two hours to clean up the mess in the kitchen.

"So the way I figure it," Opera said while digging out the last few kernels of popcorn from behind the refrigerator, "God's not interested in getting material stuff. He can make stuff any old time."

"So what does He want?"

Having found three or four kernels, Opera quickly scarfed them down. "What He wants is for you to do things."

"Do things?"

"Yeah, you know, good deeds."

Suddenly the lights came on. "Of course," I said, "how could I have been so stupid?"

"Lots of practice?" he offered.

I shot him a look and began pacing. "No wonder Bartholomew never showed up. He wasn't interested in material junk, he wants me to do good deeds."

"That's right," Opera said, as he stooped down to look under the stove to check for more hidden goodies.

"Like helping people by doing super-good things."

"And volunteering for everything."

"And giving away all my money." I glanced at the clock and was hit by a wave of panic. "But it's nine o'clock in the morning! Christmas Eve is tonight!"

"So?"

"So I'm flat broke and can't think of a single really good deed I've ever done."

"Not yet," Opera said, grabbing a lone kernel behind Mom's little portable TV and gleefully devouring it. (Who needs a vacuum cleaner, when you have Opera?) "But if we hurry you can still squeeze in something."

"Like what?"

"Come on!"

First he grabbed a pencil and pad.

"What's that for?" I asked.

"If you're going to do good deeds, it's a good idea to keep a record—just in case He asks."

Next he grabbed Mom's camera. "Doesn't hurt to document your actions with photos," he explained.

After calling Wall Street and asking her to have all the loot in the driveway picked up and returned, I joined Opera out on the streets for our mission to do the greatest super-good-deeds imaginable. The way I figured it, I had less than twelve hours. Twelve hours to be as good as any human being could possibly be.

I just hoped the town was ready because, like it or not, Saint Wally was about to strike!

Chapter 7

Helpful Hands

Before I knew it, we were once again approaching the busy intersection in front of Hockeldorf's Supermarket.

"Okay," I said to Opera. "Good Deed Number One: I'm not going inside Mr. Hockeldorf's place."

"Why not?"

"I don't think his heart can take the strain . . . besides, he's probably got all his eggnog and Christmas Party Mix restacked."

"Check," Opera said, quickly writing it down.

"Oh, and we're using my pencil and paper instead of yours so that's Good Deed Number Two."

He looked at me. "That's stretching it a bit, isn't it?"

"I need all the points I can get."

He nodded. "Check. And this paper's recyclable," he added.

"Check," I said.

"And don't forget you're telling me about these good deeds in English so I don't have to translate them from a foreign language."

I looked at him. "English is the only language I know."

"Correct, but you could have learned another language and spoken in that, which would have made things much more difficult for me."

"But I didn't."

"Which means you get another good deed point," he said, marking it down.

And then I saw her. She was standing beside us at the corner . . . the queen mother of all good-deed-point makers. It was the little old lady from the supermarket and, what luck . . . Poodikens was on a leash beside her.

I strolled up beside her and grinned. "Hi, there."

She looked up smiling . . . until she recognized me.

"Sorry about yesterday," I shrugged, still trying to look pleasant.

She pulled Poodikens closer.

"So, uh, are you trying to cross this street?"

The lady ignored me and looked straight ahead. Poodikens whimpered.

Now I figured I had two choices: I could stand there doing nothing as all my valuable time was slipping by, or I could make my move and start scoring the big points. I went for the points.

"Here," I said, taking her arm, "allow me."

Before she could respond, I helped her off the curb. I looked over my shoulder and smiled for the photo opportunity with Opera and Mom's camera. Then I continued helping the little old lady across the street. Unfortunately, she wasn't as grateful as I had hoped. In fact, she seemed downright hostile.

Granted, it might have had something to do with the "Don't Walk" sign flashing across the street. But, as you may recall, those types of details don't mean much, especially when you're busy scoring points to impress God.

She kept shouting something, but it was hard to hear anything over the yapping of her dog, much less the honking horns, screeching tires, and swearing drivers. Interestingly enough it was the same honking, screeching, and swearing that I'd heard the day before. As much as I wanted to stick around and talk over old times with my driver buddies, I didn't have a second to waste. So, with a friendly wave to my fans, we continued across the street to the other side.

The best I can figure is that the woman had never experienced such kindness because, when we finally reached the curb, she was absolutely speechless. Oh, she moved her mouth and everything, but no sounds came. Nothing but pathetic wheezes and squeaks.

"That's okay," I said, "no need to thank me. It's all in a day's work." The words had barely left my mouth before I turned and spotted our next victim, er, person in need. . . .

It was a bell-ringing Santa Claus just down the street. From the looks of the cast on his leg, he must have been the one I ran into the day before.

"Hi there," I grinned as we approached. "Remember me?"

His response was the same as the little old lady's. Wide, terrified eyes. He moved closer to his little pot of money and rang his bell louder.

"Sorry about yesterday," I shouted over the noise.

He rang the bell harder and louder. Instead of a plea for donations it almost sounded like a cry for help. I shook off the silly thought.

"So . . ." I yelled, "where does all this money you're raising go?"

Looking frantically about, he rang the bell even faster and louder.

Opera shouted to me. "Can't you read?" He pointed to a little sign. "It says here that it's to help the poor and needy."

My eyes lit up. "That's great," I shouted back. "That means if we help him, we're actually helping *lots* of people, right?"

Opera nodded. He raised his camera to get another picture while I went into action.

"Hey, Mister," I shouted to a passing man with a briefcase and overcoat. "How come you're not giving any money to this Santa here?"

The man looked up, startled.

"You ought to be able to afford something."

The man looked away and tried to get past, but I sort of blocked his path, so he had to stop.

"Come on," I shouted. "Don't be a Scrooge—it's Christmas!"

By now other people were starting to stare. The guy glanced around embarrassed. Normally I'd be embarrassed, too, but not nearly as embarrassed as showing up at Jesus' birthday party without a gift.

"Dig deep," I urged, "You can afford it!"

He still hesitated.

I was getting desperate. There had to be some way to make him see reason. And then, don't ask me why, but I suddenly remembered another one of those old movies. The one where the good guy holds off the bad guy by shoving his hand into his pocket and pretending it's a gun. It seemed innocent enough, and maybe a little comedy would help this fellow get my point. So I gave it a try.

"Come on, now," I grinned. "Hand it over."

My plan worked perfectly. The guy forked over everything he had. Loose change, bills, even his credit cards. It couldn't have been better, except for the part where he didn't know I was joking. Or where the policeman saw us, hauled us off to jail, and we had to do some fast talking to finally get out. (Unfortunately, they didn't go quite so easy on the Santa, but that's okay. They said they serve real cool meals in jail on Christmas.)

Finally, there was the canned food drive put on by the Hard Hat Construction Company. . . .

You really can't blame me for that one. After all, it was Opera who saw the location of it in the newspaper. It was the owner of the company who thought it would be a good gimmick to stack the cans in a dump truck. And it was my God-given clumsiness that caused me to accidentally trip the Dump Lever. . . .

I'll save you the gory details. Let's just say it was quite a sight watching all 302,123 cans of food spill out of the truck and roll down Main Street. In fact, the newspaper said it was the third worst traffic jam in the city's history. (The first two had taken place earlier that day and yesterday morning in front of Hockeldorf's Supermarket.)

Yes sir, it was good to see my old brake-screeching and horn-honking buddies again. It was even better when the owner of Hard Hat Construction gave us each a twenty-dollar bill and begged us to go home before we tried to help him anymore.

* * * * *

But time was running out. It was 2:30 P.M. In less than ten hours, I'd be back in dreamland. In ten hours, I'd be at the party. In ten hours, I'd be holding a dazzling list of . . . of . . . "What?" I asked impatiently as we threw open my door and raced up the stairs. "What's my total, how many Good-Deed Points do I have?"

The smell of Mom's Christmas baking filled the house, but Opera and I barely noticed as he fumbled with the photos and quickly added up the figures. "So far your number of points is . . ." he hesitated, looked up, and tried to smile. "Actually, you have a minus five."

"What??"

"A minus five."

"How's that possible?" I cried. "How could I work all day and wind up with less points than when I started!"

"I'm not sure. But I had to take something off for traumatizing the little old lady, sending Santa to jail, and destroying the canned food drive."

"But . . . but, you've messed up somewhere," I said. "Add it again."

He started again as we reached the top of the stairs and headed toward my room. We had to step over Carrie and Collision, who were busy practicing for the Christmas pageant. At the moment, Carrie was using a rubber band to fasten not one, but two of my brothers' discarded snow-cone cups on top of Collision's head.

"Hey, Squirt, what are you doing to Collision?"

"He's playing a sheep in the field when the angel of the Lord appears. Actually he's a ram. Those cups are his horns."

Collision looked to me mournfully.

I felt kinda sorry for him and made a suggestion. "Don't you think you should have taken the snow out of those cones before putting them on him?"

"Is that why he's shivering?"

"Could be. Probably explains the pretty shade of blue he's turning, too."

"Oh." Carrie nodded. Then with the half-second attention span of a six-year-old, she immediately changed the subject. "So are you going to help me with my lines now?"

"We're really pressed for time, Squirt. Maybe tomorrow."

"But the Christmas pageant is *tonight*."

I glanced to Opera. He was still adding up (or was it subtracting down) my points. I sighed as loudly as I could—for, as we all know, if you're going to be put out helping a sister, it's best she know how much. That way you can hold it over

her head the next time you need a favor. "Okay,"
I said, "what's the problem?"

She handed me a wadded-up piece of paper. "I'm
supposed to say these words and point to the angels
in the sky."

"So what's the problem?"

"I'm not sure which angel is which."

"What do you mean?"

"I'm supposed to say, 'Lo and Behold, the angels
of the Lord.'"

"And?"

"I'm not sure which angel is Lo and which angel
is Behold."

I threw a glance to Opera. He succeeded in not
laughing, but did manage to mutter, "Like brother,
like sister."

"No Squirt," I said, bending down to her. "*Lo*
and *Behold* aren't their names. That's just an
expression they used in the Bible."

"*Expression?*"

"Yeah, you know like, 'Check it out,' or, 'He's too
cool,' or, or . . .'"

"Or 'Wally, the Dorkoid'?" she asked helpfully.

There was more snickering from my point-
keeper.

"Well, sort of, yeah. The thing is, you point to
all of the angels, not to just Lo and Behold."

"Thanks," she grinned, rising up and giving me

a peck on the cheek. "You're the best big brother
a sister ever had."

"Right," I said, discreetly wiping it off. "Just
don't let it get around, all right?"

She gave me another smile, grabbed Collision
by his snow-cone horns, and took off down the hall
to work on her new interpretation of the part.

"Hey, Wally." Opera finally looked up from his
pad. "You were right. I did make a mistake on
these points."

"See."

"I dropped a zero."

"Thought so."

"It's not a minus 5, it's a minus 50."

"What?!"

He showed me the figures. Of course he was
right, so of course I began to pace.

"Oh, man, what am I supposed to do? It's almost
three o'clock. Christmas Eve is just around the
corner and I've got nothing."

"You still have a little time," Opera said.

I kept pacing. "I tried buying Him stuff, but that
didn't work. I tried doing good deeds, that didn't
help either."

"What about money?"

"You mean giving all my money to the poor?"

"Exact-a-mundo."

"Opera, I'm flat broke."

He glanced at his watch. "We've still got a few hours to make some dough."

"What are you talking—"

"At Pederson's Hobby and Sporting Goods Store. I have to catch the bus and be there in 15 minutes, and we still need reindeer." He grabbed my arm. "Come on."

"But . . . you said they barely pay you."

"Barely pay is better than no pay."

We headed downstairs. I managed to leave a note for Mom and grab ol' Betsy before heading out.

"Yeah, but $4.50 an hour?" I complained.

"And all the Trail Mix you can eat . . ."

"Yeah, but . . ."

"With honey-roasted peanuts . . . don't forget the honey-roasted peanuts."

Oh yes, the honey-roasted peanuts. How could I forget?

Chapter 8

Reindeer Bronco Busting

Opera and I caught the Number 11 Bus and headed for Pederson's Hobby and Sporting Goods Store. I had nothing against making $4.50 an hour. Actually I figured that was a pretty good rate since I normally scored a whole 75 cents an hour for helping Mom pull weeds. Then, of course, there's Dad's great rates. During the blistering heat of summer all I had to do was fight and sweat and slave with the lawn mower for a few dozen hours and I'd get a whopping $3.25!

So believe me, $4.50 wasn't bad. But $4.50 times just a few hours did not make for a really swell, knock-you-out present for God's Only Son. Needless to say, I wasn't thrilled about the deal. I was even less thrilled about having to dress up as a reindeer and prance around in some window display.

"It'll be fun," Opera insisted. "If none of the other reindeer show up, maybe they'll let you be Rudolph."

"Rudolph?" I asked.

"Yeah, you'd get to wear a battery-operated nose that lights up and everything."

I groaned. "Great."

"Hey," he grinned, "what are friends for? By the way, have you thought about which charity you'll give the money to?"

"Which one do you think will impress Jesus the most?"

"Well, there's always the fight against world hunger."

"That's good."

"And there's plenty of homeless people to help."

"That's good, too."

"Or . . ."

"Or what?"

"Pay for the therapy sessions that little old lady with the poodle has to go through, or send bail money to get the Santa out of jail, or pay for the lawsuits Hard Hat Construction is getting for all the wrecked cars those rolling cans caused."

"Good ideas," I sighed. "That way maybe I can at least get my score back up to zero."

I looked out the window and thought about Bartholomew. I sure hoped he understood all

the trouble I was going to. And, more importantly,
when we went to heaven tonight, I hoped he'd put
in a good word for me.

To take my mind off my worries, I reached down
and pulled out ol' Betsy. Might as well see what
Bubblegum Man was up to:

When we last left our gummy chum he
was busy tracking down the gruesome and
probably pretty grimy Gravity Guy.

Unfortunately, Bubblegum Man had just
run into a little thing called water,
actually a gazillion gallons of it. Even
that wasn't a problem, except for the
part about swimming.

He can't.

But, as you may recall (since your
brilliant author mentioned it earlier)
Bubblegum Man has already turned himself into a giant bubble. So, before he
has a chance to breathe in too much
water, he bobs to the surface and looks
around.

The city is worse than he expects.
The parts not under water still don't
have gravity. High school pole vaulters
are shooting themselves to the moon,

elevators keep rising past their top floors, weight-loss clinics are going out of business.

And then he hears it:

"Moo-who-who-ha-ha-he-he!"

It's coming from the Convention Center, directly below him.

Stretching his legs all the way to the earth, Bubblegum Man's sticky feet stick to the front steps. Then, with super-human effort, he pulls himself down to the ground, races to the doors, and throws them open, only to discover...

Oh no! It's the International Cat's Cradle Competition. Everywhere he looks there are girls weaving string between their fingers, trading it back and forth, making these incredibly ugly designs they think are so keen.

But that's not the bad news. The bad news is that all of their yarn has floated off their hands and the only thing they have left to string with is ...you guessed it:

"GET HIM!" Gravity Guy shouts.

Before Bubblegum Man has a chance to figure out what you've already figured, the girls grab him and start stretching

him longer and longer until he's nothing but a thin string...exactly what
they need to finish their contest.

Soon he's stretched out all over the
arena (talk about spreading yourself
too thin). But that's okay, because
he's the hero of this story, and heroes
always come up with something. It's
in their contracts.

"Ladies," he cries, "ladies, may I
have your attention."

All the chatter dies down to a mind-
less roar.

"You all know that despite my heroically
handsome features, I'm actually a piece
of bubblegum."

"So?" they say.

"So what do people do with bubblegum?"

"They chew it."

"Precisely. That means I've probably
been inside somebody's mouth. Maybe
even a boy's."

"OOOOO...GROSS...GAG..." they scream.

"That is until they spit me out..."

"OOOOO...DOUBLE GROSS...DOUBLE GAG..."

"...and left me all gooey and slobbery."

"AUGHHHH!!!"

It was the slobbery part that got

them. Suddenly everyone drops our hero onto the floor and races to the restroom to wash their hands. Girls, go figure.

In a flash, Bubblegum Man rolls himself back into a giant wad just in time to spot the badly behaving bad guy making like a cheap pair of jeans and splitting.

Bubblegum Man follows Gravity Guy out the exit just in time to catch a glimpse of him crossing the street and entering a barbershop. Bubblegum Man grins. Having read ahead in this story, he knows there is no other doorway. At last, he has Gravity Guy cornered.

He races across the street and throws open the doors only to discover...

OH NO, NOT AGAIN...cut hair is floating everywhere. Some of it bleached, some of it permed, some of it buzzed. But it makes no difference how the hair came off, the point is it's all going back on...on to Bubblegum Man!

Before he knows it, our hero has turned into the world's biggest hairball. Any place there's a sticky spot on his body (which is everywhere) there is hair. He can no longer see, he can no longer walk, he can no longer do anything.

Gravity Guy lets go with another one
of his "Moo-who-who-ha-ha-he-he!"
laughs as he hops off his Anti-Gravity
Generator and grabs a razor. "Give it
up, Chewy Chump, it's all over."

"Morrfphporporph," Bubblegum Man
says. (You'd say Morrfphporporph, too,
if your tongue was covered in hair.)

Closer and closer Gravity Man
approaches, checking the sharpness of
the razor and sneering, "Looks like
this is one shave that may be too
close."

And then, just as all appears lost,
our superhero has a super idea.
Suddenly he—

"Let's go, Wally," Opera said, rising to his feet.

I looked up. The bus had come to a stop in front
of Pederson's Hobby and Sporting Goods Store.
Outside, little kids had their little kids' noses
pressed to the display window, watching and waiting for their big moment to hang out with Santa
. . . and, of course, his trusty reindeer.

Reluctantly, I shut off ol' Betsy and followed
Opera down the bus aisle to face whatever awaited
me. . . .

* * * * *

Actually the job wasn't too bad, if you don't mind wearing a reindeer suit that looks (and smells) like it was made from old, worn out, brown carpet. The white spray-painted chest was also a nice touch, though I would have appreciated it more if they'd painted it *before* I put it on.

And what reindeer costume would be complete without antlers? But these were no fake foam antlers. Oh no, that would have been too easy. Since they wanted to go for a realistic look, they attached real antlers (which only weighed slightly less than 300 pounds) to something like an old World War I flying cap. This was carefully tied under my chin so the whole getup wouldn't wobble and fall all over the place. Of course, that didn't stop my head from wobbling and falling all over the place, but once I got the hang of it, it wasn't too bad.

What was bad was the nose.

"Isn't it cool?" Opera asked, as he busily slipped into his Santa outfit. "I told you if nobody else showed up, you'd get to play Rudolph."

Mr. Pederson, the balding store owner, had just plopped a red, round cup (the size of a well-fed tennis ball) over my nose. That wasn't the bad part. The bad part was its battery-powered glow—a glow so bright that I couldn't seen anything else.

But that's okay. I was just a reindeer. I really didn't need to see anything else. Just the artificial grass I was supposed to graze on.

We got into position behind the window. I was on the fake grass beside the fake Christmas tree with the fake snow, and Opera was climbing into his gas-powered Quad Runner, a four wheeler that was supposed to pass for a sleigh. (They would have used a real sleigh, but since they just happened to be selling this exact model of Quad Runners at a reduced price, for some unexplained reason they decided to use it instead. Go figure.)

I asked Opera, "Are they going to let you drive that home when you're done?"

"I could," Opera snickered. "All I'd have to do is turn on this key here, and away we'd go."

"Okay, Santa, cut the chatter," Mr. Pederson growled. "We've got a lot of kids to see you and less than three hours before we close." With that he opened the gate, and in they swarmed.

Ah, childhood. So sweet, so innocent. What a treat it was to hear the titter of their delicate little voices. . . .

I WANT THIS! . . . I WANT THAT! . . . YOU'RE NOT A REAL REINDEER! . . . DO THESE ANTLERS COME OFF? . . . WHAT ABOUT THIS NOSE? . . . HEY, THIS SNOW IS FAKE!

Doing my best to remember that this Santa and reindeer act was for a good cause, I ignored the little buggers and continued my artificial grass-eating routine . . . until one of the cute little monsters thought it would be great fun to ride a reindeer.

Without warning, he leaped onto my back. No problem, I thought. I can play horsey with the best of them. Then came Monsters #2, #3, #4, and #5.

It was #5 that did it. Actually it wasn't the kid, it was his spurs. Having just come from the toy department, his mommy and daddy had evidently thought it would be swell to buy him a pair of make-believe cowboy boots with not-so-make-believe spurs.

"Giddie up!" he shouted, driving the spurs hard into my side.

"YEOW!" I cried, leaping up. Normally with five kids on your back, leaping up is not an easy feat, but with three-inch spurs inbedded in your side, it's amazing how you can find the motivation.

The other kids slid off, but not #5. He hung on for dear life, jabbing his spurs in even deeper.

"Ride 'em, cowboy!" Monster boy cried.

"Oh, isn't he cute!" his mommy beamed.

"Rudolph, hold still while I take a picture," his daddy ordered.

But holding still was not what I had in mind.

I twirled around, trying to throw off the little buckaroo, but he dug in even harder again and again and again some more.

I twirled and spun even faster. And then it happened. I'm not sure of the details, but it began with crashing into the fake Christmas tree. Then, getting my antlers tangled up in the tree's Christmas lights. Then, jumping back and pulling out all the lights so they were now hanging from my antlers.

But that was child's play compared to my next little feat. After tap dancing on a few kids . . .

"Mommy, Rudolph is attacking me!"

Knocking over a few parents . . .

"My back! I'll sue! I'll sue!"

And basically destroying all of the decorations in the display (while still feeling the "gentle caress" of spurs jabbing my rib cage) . . .

"Ride 'em, cowboy!"

"Oh, this is just darling!"

"Rudolph, please hold still!"

I finally crashed into a wall. Unfortunately, this was no ordinary wall. This was the wall that held the store's circuit breaker box. No problem, I thought, just as long as I don't trip and . . .

"Oops!"

That was me tripping.

CRASH

That was me falling into the circuit breakers
with my electrically wired antlers.

SNAP, CRACKLE, FIZZLE, FIZZLE, POP

That was the entire circuit box shorting out. A
feat impossible for normal people, but thanks to
my electrical training from Dad, it was a breeze.

I had managed to put out all the overhead lights
in the store. Everything was dark . . . except for
the sparks flying everywhere. But light or dark,
it didn't matter. With the red, battery-powered
glow in front of my eyes, I couldn't see a thing.

I staggered forward, smashing a few more little darlings along the way, until I finally stumbled over Opera and landed at his feet. Ah, at last
a friend. Someone I could turn to in my time of
trouble. Someone who's gentle understanding
would—

"Wally, quit being a jerk."

I grabbed the Quad Runner to pull myself up
and . . .

"Wally, don't turn that key! You'll . . ."

I accidentally turned the key, and . . .

"Wally!"

. . . fired up the Quad, and . . .

"WALLLLLLLYYYYY! . . ."

. . . off we went. Monster Boy on top of me, me
on top of Opera, and Opera on his gasoline
powered sleigh.

"Ride 'em, cowboy!" shouted Monster Boy.

"Oh, this is so precious!" said his mommy.

"Rudolph, will you *please* hold still!" said his daddy.

Then came Opera's hysterical screaming. "I hope you're done horsing around, 'cause I can't shut this thing off!"

Chapter 9

Chaos Rains

The three of us roared down the dark aisle, screaming our heads off. I know it isn't polite to scream
in public, but I doubt anybody noticed since they
were all too busy leaping out of the way and
screaming their own heads off.

"Shut this thing down!" I yelled.

"I can't!" Opera yelled back. "You broke off the
key!"

BAMB!

"Sorry, Sir," I shouted.

BANG!

"Sorry, Ma'am," Opera cried.

BARK, SQUEAL, SQUEAL.

"What was that?" I yelled.

"Your little old lady friend and her poodle!"

"Oh, no. . . . She sure gets around!"

"Not anymore!"

Since two's company and three's a crowd, the first to go was my little buckaroo buddy. I'm not exactly sure when we lost him, though I suspect it was when we zoomed up the down escalator (those steps can be a bit bumpy . . . so can those poor shoppers who had no place to jump out of the way).

Next stop was the Sporting Goods Department.

"What's that?" Opera pointed.

I squinted. The headlights caught something dead ahead. "It looks like—"

K-BAMB!

Baseballs and pieces of machinery flew everywhere.

"It was a pitching machine," I cried as we banked off the back wall and started to double back. "We hit a pitching machine!"

"No problem!" he shouted. "Just as long as we didn't accidentally turn it—"

SMACK

"OW!"

"What's wrong?"

"Somebody hit me!"

SMACK

"OW!"

SMACK

"OW!"

"That's not a somebody," I shouted. "Those are . . ."

SMACK

"OW!"

". . . baseballs. We've turned on the . . ."

SMACK

"OW!"

SMACK

"OW!"

". . . pitching machine!"

Baseballs flew in every direction.

SMACK

"OW!"

Well, not every direction. Just at . . .

SMACK

"OW!"

. . . us.

"Wally, duck!"

"What?"

"I said—"

THUNK!

That was us passing under the bars of a weight-lifting machine. Actually it was Opera passing under the bars. I was a little busy being knocked to the floor totally unconscious.

When I finally came to, the store was still in the dark. By the sound of things, most of the people had managed to escape. I rose unsteadily to my feet and noticed . . .

SMACK

"OW!"

. . . the pitching machine was still going. I

dropped to my hoofs and knees as the balls flew overhead.

SWISH, SWISH, SWISH

It was like an old war movie where the guy crawls forward keeping his head down so it doesn't become Swiss cheese. I don't know how long I crawled, but the baseballs . . .

SWISH, SWISH, SWISH

. . . just kept coming. After about three and a half miles of crawling, I noticed the balls . . .

SWISH, SWISH, SWISH

. . . had never lost any speed. They came as fast as ever. Something was wrong. It was about this time that I looked down and noticed I hadn't been crawling on the floor, but on a treadmill. Great. No wonder I never got anywhere. I had wasted all my time crawling on the stupid machine (though I'm sure the exercise was great for my cardiovascular system).

Finally, I stood up . . .

SMACK

"OW!"

. . . got back down, and made a beeline for . . .

"WOAH!" *THUMP.* "OW!" *BUMP.* "OUCH!" *BOUNCE, BOUNCE, BOUNCE.*

It looked like I'd found the escalator again. It's great when you finally get to know your way around a place.

After a few more *THUMPS* and *BUMPS* and a couple *BOUNCES* thrown in for good measure, I finally hit the bottom. I knew I was back in the toy department, not because of my uncanny sense of direction, but because . . .

ROLL, ROLL, ROLL, ROLL . . .

that's where they kept the skateboards. I was sprawled spread eagle, across half a dozen of them, rolling down a side aisle at just under the speed of sound. Fortunately, most of the shoppers had made it out of the store (or had already been hospitalized from the last time I swung by this department) so there were no major problems . . . except with my stakeboarding skills. Always doing my best to hide any athletic ability, I only managed to stay on the boards a couple of seconds before crashing into a giant Nintendo display case.

The good news was I didn't even crack the glass. The bad news was I cracked me. I tried to stand but only fell backwards, smack dab in the middle of the main aisle.

I lay there on my back, killing time by counting my broken bones, as I waited for the next catastrophe to strike. But nothing more happened. No falling shelves, no collapsing roofs. Not even a major hurricane or earthquake. Nothing.

Was I losing my touch? Was it over so soon?

Slowly I rolled onto my stomach and rose to what was left of my hands and knees.

And then I saw the light . . .

But we're not talking God or Bartholomew or anything like that. We're talking about Opera and his runaway Quad Runner.

"WALLY!"

Between the glare of my red nose and the glare of his headlight, it was impossible to see exactly where he was heading. But I knew the general direction.

Roughly, I'd say he was generally heading TOWARD ME!

"LOOK OUT!"

I dodged to the left. But since great minds think alike that was exactly where he turned. So I spun to the right. Repeat performance.

My goose was cooked. My turkey stuffed. My cranberries, uh, cranberried. (That should do it for Christmas dinner metaphors.) The point was, my whole life passed before my eyes. Well, not really—that would have been too painful. And by the looks of things, I was about to experience enough pain for several lifetimes.

I managed to think that here I had spent all my time working to get Jesus a cool present and what was my reward? Winding up as some sort of reindeer road kill.

I'll save you the ugly details . . . like how I jumped to the right one last time which is exactly the direction Opera swerved. Or how the impact completely shorted out my glowing nose which sent sparks in all directions and sent me sailing into the air like a punted football.

I will mention, however, that I never hit the floor. Instead, I managed to land on top of the neck of Darryl, the giant, fifteen-foot bobbing duck.

What joy! What luck!

Except for the bobbing up and down part. The bobbing down was no problem. It was when we bobbed up that we ran into difficulty. Darryl's neck was tall, almost reaching to the ceiling. And since the ceiling was where they kept the smoke detectors, and since my little electrical nose was still smoldering . . . well, it was just a matter of seconds before the automatic sprinklers kicked in and the entire store experienced the world's biggest indoor rainstorm.

By the looks of things it was over. It had to be. I'd run out of bones to break and merchandise to ruin. I don't know how long I lay there bobbing up and down as the water washed over me. I do remember praying that the manager would forget that he had guns and live ammunition upstairs in the Sporting Goods Department.

Finally, I heard somebody climbing up Darryl

the Duck's leg, then felt that somebody climbing onto my back . . . a somebody who just happened to be wearing spurs!

There was a bright flash and then the all-too-familiar voices:

"Ride 'em, cowboy . . ."

"Oh, that's so precious . . ."

"Thank you, Mr. Rudolph. We'll cherish this picture always."

* * * * *

Later that evening, after Mr. Pederson admitted it was actually his fault (he was the one foolish enough to hire me), I finally arrived home and joined my family around the Christmas tree.

Everything was just as Mom had planned—the tree, the food, the candlelight, the carols she played on the piano, the crackling fireplace . . . and, most importantly, all of us pitching in to help decorate the tree.

At the moment Dad was dumping more wood onto the fire, Burt and Brock were hanging the lights, and Carrie and I were setting up the miniature manger scene on the coffee table. (I had volunteered to give my brothers a hand, but due to my recent electrical experiences, Dad thought it best to keep me away from anything that had a plug on it.)

As Carrie unwrapped the wise men and handed them to me, I said, "Sorry about missing your pageant tonight. How'd it go?"

"Great," she beamed. "Mrs. Snickelstern said I was the best shepherd in the whole play."

"No kidding?" I said. "You didn't have any problems with the angels?"

"Not a one—except for the part where Billy Bartelson, who played another shepherd, accidentally hit Matthew Martin, who played Gabriel, over the head with his cane and knocked him out."

"Billy Bartelson did that?"

"Yeah. Mrs. Snickelstern was wondering if you'd been giving him private lessons or anything."

"No," I said, trying to smile, "but it's nice to know somebody's following in my footsteps."

I took the angel that Carrie had handed me and stared at it. In just an hour or so I'd be meeting Bartholomew again. That is, if he even bothered to show up. And, once again, I'd have nothing to show him. Once again I'd have nothing to offer Jesus on His birthday.

I took a deep breath and fought back the lump that was trying to grow in my throat.

I had failed. Big time. First, by thinking I could buy Jesus something. Then by overdosing on good-deed-doing. And finally, by trying to earn money for Him.

Everything I had tried had failed. The lump in

my throat grew bigger. I took an angry swipe at
my eyes. For some reason they were starting to
burn and fill with tears. I concentrated with all my
might to keep them dry and was doing a pretty
good job . . . until Mom started singing at the piano:

> "Silent night, Holy night.
> All is calm, all is bright."

One by one the rest of the family joined in.

> "'Round yon virgin, mother and child.
> Holy infant so tender and mild."

I stared at the carpet so no one would see my
tears. No one but Carrie. Maybe that's why she
pressed in closer to my side. Maybe that's why
she reached out and took my hand.

> "Sleep in heavenly peace.
> Sleep in heavenly peace."

Of course, she was clueless at what I was going
through. But that didn't seem to matter. I was her
big brother, and she loved me—no matter how
many Hobby and Sporting Goods stores I destroyed,
or angels I disappointed, or gifts I was unable to
give to Jesus.

I glanced up through my tears. There were Burt and Brock over by the tree, singing just as out of key as always. But no one cared about that, either. After all, they were family, and we loved them regardless of all their superjockiness.

> "Silent night, Holy night.
> Shepherds quake at the sight."

Beside my brothers stood Dad. Maybe not the world's best artist when it comes to outdoor lighting, but loved by us as if he were a Rembrandt.

And, finally, over at the piano sat Mom—the one everyone takes for granted . . . the one who never seems to stop working . . . and by far the greatest example of someone who will never stop loving her family, no matter what.

Because that's what we were . . . a family. A family that, despite all of our strengths and weaknesses, still loved one another. No matter how we failed, no matter how we succeeded, we were loved.

> "Glories stream from heaven afar,
> Heavenly hosts sing alleluia;"

As I looked around at my family, I realized it made no difference whether I succeeded or failed.

They would always be there for me. They would always love me. I took a deep breath and closed my eyes. I may have failed everybody else, I may have failed Bartholomew, maybe even God . . . but I was still loved. And, at least for tonight, that made all the difference in the world.

> "Christ, the Savior is born,
> Christ, the Savior is born."

Chapter 10

Wrapping Up

"Wallace? I say, Wallace, old man, I'm on a bit of a schedule, here. May we please get on with this dream?"

Recognizing the voice, I pried open my eyes and saw I was back in the motorcycle shop. Only this time there were no movie stars waiting in line for my autograph and no hot bikes waiting to be bought by my mom. It was just me sitting at the counter in the deserted shop . . . and Bartholomew, in his white tuxedo, top hat, and cane, looking as neat and dapper as ever.

"I just stopped by for a moment to congratulate you."

"Congratulate me?"

"Yes. The Lord is very pleased with the presents you sent up to Him."

I blinked. "Would you run that past me again?"

"He said your gifts were some of the nicest ones He's received all season."

My mind raced, trying to figure out what Bartholomew was talking about. Could it have been all that stuff I'd bought at the mall? Was it possible that Wall Street hadn't returned them and that they somehow made it into heaven?

As if reading my mind, Bartholomew laughed. "Don't be foolish, Wallace. What would the good Lord do with a tablesaw, basketball shoes, and a giant screen TV?"

"What about the recliner with built-in Cheez Whiz spreader?"

"Hmm," he thought a moment. "I'll have to run that one past Him."

"But if it's not all the stuff I bought, then are you talking about all those good deeds I did?"

"Nearly giving that little old lady a heart attack, landing the bell-ringing Santa in jail, destroying the canned food drive—those hardly amount to good deeds, do they, Wallace?"

"But that only leaves my trying to make money at Pederson's Hobby and Sporting Goods Store. And, after destroying the place, I didn't have the guts to ask Mr. Pederson to pay me."

"Actually, we were all impressed with your wisdom in not asking him for money—with all those guns and live ammunition he has up in the Sporting Goods Department."

"Then what?" I asked. "What's left? What did I—"

"What did you give Jesus?"

I nodded.

Bartholomew leaned on his cane and looked me squarely in the eyes. "You gave Him a gift from your heart, Wallace. That was the gift that touched Him."

I frowned, still not understanding.

"All those other things are important . . . donating material goods, helping people, giving money to charities—those are excellent endeavors and ones you must always remember to do."

"But I offered all of those things, and He didn't accept any of them."

"Because you gave them with the wrong attitude. You gave them out of obligation. You gave them to be religious."

"He doesn't like religious?"

Bartholomew shook his head. "No. He likes love. And it was your reaching out to others in love that really touched Him."

"I'm sorry, I still don't understand."

Without a word he reached over and tapped a portable TV that was on the countertop. A portable TV that looked exactly like the one in Mom's kitchen.

An image flickered on the screen. It was a klutzy kid out on the front lawn trying to help his dad with outdoor lights. A klutzy kid that, from all his stumbling and bumbling around, could only be . . .

"Hey, that's me!" I cried.

"Precisely."

"But helping Dad with the lights wasn't important. I was just trying to give him a hand."

"It may not be important to you, but it was important to your Dad. And because it was important to him, it was important to God."

Bartholomew tapped the screen. There I was again. Only this time, swimming through the popcorn trying to turn off the microwave for Burt and Brock.

"He found this particularly touching."

"But those were just my brothers."

"Correct. And what you did for them, you were doing for God."

Another tap, another picture. There I was standing on the stairs giving Carrie drama lessons about the angels Lo and Behold.

"Helping Carrie counts?" I asked.

"You did it in love, didn't you?"

"Well, yeah, but . . ."

"Then you did it for God."

Finally he touched the screen one last time, and there we all were, decorating the tree and singing Silent Night. It was almost as moving watching it on TV as it was being there—well, except for my brothers' singing.

But what really got me was the expression on Mom's face. There was no way to describe her joy as she sat there playing the piano. There was no way to describe the look of love in her eyes.

I cleared my throat. "Last night was really important to her, wasn't it?"

Bartholomew nodded. "And because it was important to her, it was important to the Lord."

I continued staring at the screen as Bartholomew began to put on his gloves. "So you see, Wally, God is not interested in your saying and doing things for Him out of fear or obligation or being religious. He's interested in your living with His love in your heart. A love you can best express by loving others. Because what you do for others . . ."

I nodded, finishing the phrase, ". . . you do for God."

"Good show," Bartholomew said, tapping his hat and preparing to leave.

Suddenly, I remembered something. "But wait a minute," I cried. "You promised me I could go to Jesus' birthday party."

"And so you did."

"When . . .where?"

"Last night, in your living room."

I looked back at the TV screen where we were still singing Silent Night. "But Jesus wasn't there."

"Oh yes He was, Wallace. For, wherever people who love Him are gathered, there He is, too. And if you hurry and get some sleep you will be rested to continue that party."

"You mean it's going to keep going?"

"Absolutely. Christmas morning is just around the corner. You will have the entire day to continue attending His party. Now go back to sleep." Bartholomew started to fade.

"But Bartholomew . . ." The lump in my throat was coming back. "How can I ever thank you?"

"Oh I'm not the one to thank, ol' bean." He threw a look to heaven. "I think you know who should be thanked."

"But . . . how can I thank Him?"

"Just keep giving Him your heart, Wallace. Just keep letting Him love you, and love others through you. That's all He really wants, old man. That's all He's ever wanted. That's the greatest gift you can ever give Him. Until next time, Ta-ta."

With that, Bartholomew was gone.

I sat all alone in the bike shop. Even though it was only a dream, I knew I had learned something very important. Something I planned never to forget . . . What I do for others I really do for God. I closed my eyes and drifted back into sleep. Christmas morning was just around the corner, and it was going to be the best Christmas I had ever had.

In fact, it already was.

* * * * *

When I woke up the next morning, it was still dark outside. Since I didn't hear any screaming, rioting, or ravaging of gifts, I figured no one was up yet. So I reached for ol' Betsy and thought I'd kill some time by finishing up my superhero story. . . .

When we last left our chewy hairball, his superstickiness had attracted every cut hair in the local barbershop. No problem. Since wads of bubblegum usually have difficulty growing hair, Bubblegum Man had actually been think-ing of buying a toupee.

However, there was another minor problem. The one where Gravity Guy was floating toward him wielding a razor as big as Omaha.

Our good guy tries to lighten the mood with a little good-guy humor. "Just take a little off the top, okay?"

But Gravity Guy sneers, "I was think-ing of taking off the whole top."

(So much for humor.)

Before Bubblegum Man can answer (or

try out his latest knock-knock joke just in case Gravity Guy didn't get that first bit of comedy), our baddest of bad guys takes three expert swipes with the razor. The first swipe shaves the hair from the top of our hero's head. The second removes all the hair on his left side, the third, all the hair on his right...though he leaves the sideburns and beard, since sideburns and beards are always cool.

Bubblegum Man has no choice. He hates to have to do what he has to do, but he has to do it. With all of his super-hero strength he manages to close his eyes and wait helplessly for the next blow.

But instead of a splitting headache, Bubblegum Man is met with the sound of a ringing bell. He glances up to see a sidewalk Santa floating overhead. Gravity Guy sees him too and lowers his razor.

"What's wrong?" our hero asks.

"I'm sorry. I don't know what came over me. I never kill, mame, or destroy anyone during Christmas."

"Why not?"

"You never know which one of your victims might be giving you a gift."

"Ah," I nodded, "good point. So Christmas means a lot to you?"

Our bad guy nods, giving a hardy, supervillain sniff. "It was the only time I was ever happy as a child." He suddenly breaks into tears.

"That's so sad," Bubblegum Man says, as he stretches his gooey arm around our bad guy's shoulders to comfort him, while carefully removing the razor, and flinging it halfway to the North Pole. Of course, it barely misses the floating Santa, but does manage to cut his beard, giving him a new appreciation of the phrase "close shave." "What about your childhood was so tough?" our superhero asks.

Gravity Guy wipes his eyes and gives another sniff. "My dad always wanted somebody to be great in sports, but I was just too short. The only thing I could do was play handball against street curbs."

"Is that why you built the Anti-Gravity Generator?"

"Yes, that way height wouldn't matter."

"But you're not too short," Bubblegum
Man encourages.

"I'm not?"

"No. Your feet reach all the way to
the ground, don't they?"

Gravity Guy looks down and brightens.
"Hey, you're right. I never thought of
that!"

"Besides," Bubblegum Man says, "if you
think you've got it bad, try being so
sticky that when people step on you,
they track you halfway across town."

"I never thought of that," Gravity Guy
says. "But at least you're tall enough
to get into your high tops without a
step ladder."

"Gee, that is tough—almost as bad as
getting stuck in some kid's braces."

And so they continue talking and
listening, growing in understanding and
compassion. Each slowly becoming friends
with the other. And, before you know it
(after Bubblegum Man offers to give
stretching lessons that will add a good
twenty or thirty feet to his height),
Gravity Guy agrees to reform and shut
down his Anti-Gravity Generator.

Everyone gently drifts back to the

ground. They begin clapping and cheering. Not only because their weight has returned, but because they can resume their frantic racing to and fro to buy Christmas gifts for one another.

So, with the help of this super-convenient and pretty mushy ending (along with swelling music that really proves it's an ending) the world becomes a safer, kinder place in which to live, chew gum, and celebrate the birth of our Savior.

I stared at the screen. It wasn't a bad ending, considering how early it was in the morning. I shut ol' Betsy down just as I heard a knock on my door.

"Come in," I said.

It was little Carrie . . . all bleary-eyed and carrying one of her thousand stuffed animals from one of those thousand most-loved Disney movies.

"What's up, Squirt?"

"It's Christmas morning."

"Yeah."

"And nobody's awake."

"It's still pretty early. I doubt anyone wants to get up yet."

"I know. But if you were to get up, and if you helped me wake up the others . . . we could start opening presents right away."

I looked at her.

"Please, Wally?"

She fidgeted, eagerly waiting for my answer. It was pretty obvious this was important to her, and after my little chat with Bartholomew and writing such a corny ending to my superhero story, how could I not help her? "Sure, Squirt," I finally said. "Why not."

"Oh, thanks, Wally!" She practically glowed as she reached up, gave me a peck on the cheek, then turned and dashed out the door with all the materialistic greed a six-year-old can muster.

I sat there a moment, smiling. Then, glancing up to heaven, I grinned.

"Happy Birthday, Jesus."

With that, I tossed off the covers, threw my feet over the bed, and fell flat on my face.

What a comfort to know that even on Christmas, some things never change. . . .

THE INCREDIBLE WORLDS OF WALLY McDOOGLE

#1—My Life As a Smashed Burrito with Extra Hot Sauce

Twelve-year-old Wally—"The walking disaster area"—is forced to stand up to Camp Wahkah Wahkah's number one all-American bad guy. One hilarious mishap follows another until, fighting together for their very lives, Wally learns the need for even his worst enemy to receive Jesus Christ. (ISBN 0-8499-3402-8)

#2—My Life As Alien Monster Bait

"Hollyweird" comes to Middletown! Wally's a superstar! A movie company has chosen our hero to be eaten by their mechanical "Mutant from Mars!" It's a close race as to which will consume Wally first—the disaster-plagued special effects "monster" or his own out-of-control pride . . . until he learns the cost of true friendship and of God's command for humility. (ISBN 0-8499-3403-6)

#3—My Life As a Broken Bungee Cord

A hot-air balloon race! What could be more fun? Then again, we're talking about Wally McDoogle, the "Human Catastrophe." Calamity builds on calamity until, with his life on the line, Wally learns what it means to FULLY put his trust in God. (ISBN 0-8499-3404-4)

#4—My Life As Crocodile Junk Food

Wally visits missionary friends in the South American rain forest. Here he stumbles onto a whole new set of impossible predicaments . . . until he understands the need and joy of sharing Jesus Christ with others.
(ISBN 0-8499-3405-2)

#5—My Life As Dinosaur Dental Floss

It starts with a practical joke that snowballs into near disaster. Risking his life to protect his country, Wally is pursued by a SWAT team, bungling terrorists, photo-snapping tourists, Gary the Gorilla, and a TV news reporter. After prehistoric-size mishaps and a talk with the President, Wally learns that maybe honesty really is the best policy. (ISBN 0-8499-3537-7)

#6—My Life As a Torpedo Test Target

Wally uncovers the mysterious secrets of a sunken submarine. As dreams of fame and glory increase, so do the famous McDoogle mishaps. Besides hostile sea creatures, hostile pirates, and hostile Wally McDoogle clumsiness, there is the war against his own greed and selfishness. It isn't until Wally finds himself on a wild ride atop a misguided torpedo that he realizes the source of true greatness. (ISBN 0-8499-3538-5)

#7—My Life As a Human Hockey Puck

Look out . . . Wally McDoogle turns athlete! Jealousy and envy drive Wally from one hilarious calamity to another until, as the team's mascot, he learns humility while suddenly being thrown in to play goalie for the Middletown Super Chickens! (ISBN 0-8499-3601-2)

#8—My Life As an Afterthought Astronaut

"Just cause I didn't follow the rules doesn't make it my fault that the Space Shuttle almost crashed. Well, okay, maybe it was sort of my fault. But not the part when Pilot O'Brien was spacewalking and I accidently knocked him halfway to Jupiter. . . ." So begins another hilarious Wally McDoogle MISadventure as our boy blunder stows aboard the Space Shuttle and learns the importance of: Obeying the Rules!
(ISBN 0-8499-3602-0)

#9—My Life As Reindeer Road Kill

Santa on an out-of-control four wheeler? Electrical Rudolph on the rampage? Nothing unusual, just Wally McDoogle doing some last-minute Christmas shopping . . . FOR GOD! Our boy blunder dreams that an angel has invited him to a birthday party for Jesus. Chaos and comedy follow as he turns the town upside down looking for the perfect gift, until he finally bumbles his way into the real reason for the Season. (ISBN 0-8499-3866-X)

#10—My Life As a Toasted Time Traveler

Wally travels back from the future to warn himself of an upcoming accident. But before he knows it, there are more Wallys running around than even Wally himself can handle. Catastrophes reach an all-time high as Wally tries to outthink God and re-write history. (ISBN 0-8499-3867-8)

#11—My Life As Polluted Pond Scum

This laugh-filled Wally disaster includes: a monster lurking in the depths of a mysterious lake . . . a glowing figure with powers to summon the creature to the shore . . . and one Wally McDoogle, who reluctantly stumbles upon the truth. Wally's entire town is in danger. He must race against the clock, his own fears, and learn to trust God before he has any chance of saving the day. (ISBN 0-8499-3875-9)

#12—My Life As a Bigfoot Breath Mint

Wally gets his big break to star with his uncle Max in the famous Fantasmo World stunt show. Unlike his father, whom Wally secretly suspects to be a major loser, Uncle Max is everything Wally longs to be . . . or so it appears. But Wally soon discovers the truth and learns who the real hero is in his life. (ISBN 0-8499-3876-7)

#13—My Life As a Blundering Ballerina

Wally agrees to switch places with Wall Street. Everyone is in on the act as the two try to survive seventy-two hours in each other's shoes and learn the importance of respecting other people. (ISBN 0-8499-4022-2)

#14—My Life As a Screaming Skydiver

Master of mayhem Wally turns a game of laser tag into international espionage. From the Swiss Alps to the African plains, Agent 00½th bumblingly employs such top-secret gizmos as rocket-powered toilet paper, exploding dental floss, and the ever-popular transformer tacos to stop the dreaded and super secret . . . Giggle Gun. (ISBN 0-8499-4023-0)

#15—My Life As a Human Hairball

When Wally and Wall Street visit a local laboratory, they are accidentally miniaturized and swallowed by some unknown stranger. It is a race against the clock as they fly through various parts of the body in a desperate search for a way out while learning how wonderfully we're made. (ISBN 0-8499-4024-9)

#16—My Life As a Walrus Whoopee Cushion

Wally and his buddies, Opera and Wall Street, win the Gazillion Dollar Lotto! Everything is great, until they realize they lost the ticket at the zoo! Add some bungling bad guys, a zoo break-in, the release of all the animals, a SWAT team or two . . . and you have the usual McDoogle mayhem as Wally learns the dangers of greed. (ISBN 0-8499-4025-7)

#17—My Life As a Mixed-Up Millennium Bug

When Wally accidentally fries the circuits of Ol' Betsy, his beloved laptop computer, suddenly whatever he types turns into reality! At 11:59, New Year's Eve, Wally tries retyping the truth into his computer—which shorts out every other computer in the world. By midnight, the entire universe has credited Wally's mishap to the MILLENNIUM BUG! Panic, chaos, and hilarity start the new century, thanks to our beloved boy blunder. (ISBN 0-8499-4026-5)

#18—My Life As a Beat-Up Basketball Backboard

Ricko Slicko's Advertising Agency claims that they can turn the dorkiest human in the world into the most popular. And who better to prove this than our boy blunder, Wally McDoogle! Soon he has his own TV series and fans wearing glasses just like his. But when he tries to be a star athlete for his school basketball team, Wally finally learns that being popular isn't all it's cut out to be. (ISBN 0-8499-4027-3)

#19—My Life As a Cowboy Cowpie

Once again our part-time hero and full-time walking disaster finds himself smack dab in another misadventure. This time it's full of dude-ranch disasters, bungling broncobusters, and the world's biggest cow—well let's just say it's not a pretty picture (or a pleasant smelling one). Through it all, Wally learns the dangers of seeking revenge. (ISBN 0-8499-5990-X)